To my beloved parents,

Your unwavering love, support, and encouragement have been the guiding lights in my life. Thank you for instilling in me a love for stories and the values they carry. This book is a tribute to the countless lessons and laughter you have gifted me throughout the years. May it bring joy and wisdom to the children who read it, just as you have brought joy and wisdom to my life.

With all my love,
Anshumali

THE SHORT STORY BOOK FOR CHILDREN - MORALS AND HUMOUR

DR ANSHUMALI PANDEY

Contents

Preface

Welcome to **"The Short Story Book for Children - Morals and Humour,"** a delightful collection of tales that blend whimsy with wisdom. In these pages, young readers will embark on enchanting adventures filled with imaginative characters and memorable lessons that resonate through time.

Stories have always been a fundamental part of our culture, allowing us to explore complex ideas through simple narratives. This book aims to engage children's curiosity while instilling essential morals that guide their behaviour and understanding of the world. Each tale encourages readers to reflect on their actions, the importance of friendship, honesty, and the value of empathy, all wrapped in the cloak of humour and charm.

From a clever crow to a dancing monkey, the characters in these stories are crafted to spark laughter and contemplation alike. We believe that the journey through literature should not only entertain but also nurture the spirit and inspire growth.

As you turn these pages with your little ones, we invite you to discuss the themes and morals embedded within each story. Together, you can discover the invaluable lessons that can shape character and understanding. May this collection inspire laughter, ignite imagination, and foster a lifelong love for reading in the hearts of young adventurers.

Happy reading!

— Dr. Anshumali Pandey

ACKNOWLEDGEMENTS

I would like to express my heartfelt gratitude to everyone who contributed to the creation of **"The Short Story Book for Children - Morals and Humour."** This book is the result of collaboration, inspiration, and encouragement from many wonderful individuals.

First and foremost, I extend my deepest thanks to my family and friends, whose unwavering support and belief in my vision provided the motivation to bring this collection to life. Your enthusiasm for storytelling has always inspired me.

I am especially grateful to the educators and mentors who have shaped my understanding of the importance of morals and humour in children's literature. Your insights have been invaluable in crafting stories that resonate with young readers and impart essential life lessons.

I would also like to acknowledge the countless authors and storytellers whose timeless fables and tales have influenced my writing. Their ability to weave wisdom into engaging narratives serves as a constant reminder of the power of storytelling.

To the illustrators and designers who have contributed their artistic talents thank you for bringing the characters and scenes to life. Your creativity enhances the reading experience and invites children into the vibrant world of imagination.

Lastly, I wish to thank the readers and their families for embarking on this journey with me. I hope these stories spark joy, laughter, and valuable discussions about life's important lessons.

ACKNOWLEDGEMENTS

Together, we can inspire the next generation of readers to appreciate the magic of stories.
With sincere appreciation,
— Dr. Anshumali Pandey

Prologue

In the enchanting realm of childhood, where imagination knows no bounds, stories have always held a special place. They are not merely tales; they are bridges to understanding the world around us. **"The Short Story Book for Children - Morals and Humour"** is a collection that aims to captivate young minds, inviting them to explore the vibrant arras of life through engaging narratives filled with humour and wisdom.

Each story within these pages serves a dual purpose: to entertain and to enlighten. They are carefully crafted to convey important life lessons that resonate with children, encouraging them to reflect on their choices and actions. From the playful antics of animals to the thoughtful musings of wise characters, these stories are designed to spark laughter and provoke thought in equal measure.

As we journey through this book, readers will meet a delightful cast of characters—daring animals, wise elders, and curious children—each offering unique insights into the joys and challenges of life. These tales remind us that every experience, whether humorous or serious, contributes to our growth and understanding.

In a world that often feels hurried and overwhelming, the stories in this collection provide a moment of pause, inviting children to laugh, learn, and appreciate the simple yet profound truths of existence. They encourage conversations between parents and children, fostering connections that deepen their understanding of the values that matter most.

As you delve into these pages, I hope you find not only enjoyment but also inspiration. May the morals woven into each story illuminate paths of kindness, honesty, and empathy, helping young readers navigate their own journeys with a smile.

Welcome to a world where humour and morals intertwine, creating a rich tapestry of stories that celebrate the essence of childhood.

Let the adventures begin!

I

The Short Story Book for Children - Morals and Humour

The Wolf and the Lamb

One day, a hungry Wolf met a little Lamb who had wandered away from its flock. The Wolf didn't want to just grab the Lamb; he wanted to make it seem like it was fair for him to eat the Lamb. So, he said, "Last year, you were very rude to me!"

The Lamb, confused, replied, "But I wasn't even born last year!" The Wolf then said, "Well, you eat from my field." The Lamb answered, "No, I haven't eaten grass yet." The Wolf tried again, "You drank from my stream!" The Lamb replied, "I haven't had water yet; I still drink my mother's milk."

Finally, the Wolf, having no more excuses, grabbed the Lamb and ate him anyway. The story teaches us that sometimes, people who are mean will always find a reason to be unfair.

The Bat and the Weasels

A Bat once fell to the ground and was caught by a Weasel. The Bat begged for his life, but the Weasel said, "I don't like birds, so I'm going to eat you." The Bat quickly replied, "But I'm not a bird, I'm a mouse!" Hearing that, the Weasel let him go.

Later, the Bat fell again and was caught by another Weasel. This time, the Weasel said, "I don't like mice, so I'm going to eat you." The Bat cleverly said, "But I'm not a mouse, I'm a bat!" And once again, the Bat was set free.

This story shows that being quick and smart can help you get out of tricky situations.

The Donkey and the Grasshopper

A Donkey once heard some Grasshoppers singing beautifully. He loved the sound so much that he wanted to sing just like them. He asked the Grasshoppers what they ate to make their voices so lovely. The Grasshoppers replied, "We eat dew from the grass."

Thinking this was the secret, the Donkey decided to eat only dew. But soon, he became very weak and died of hunger.

The lesson is that just because something works for someone else, doesn't mean it will work for you.

The Lion and the Mouse

One day, a Lion was woken up by a tiny Mouse running across his face. Angry, the Lion grabbed the Mouse and was about to eat him. The Mouse begged, "Please let me go! One day, I might be able to help you!"

The Lion laughed at the idea but decided to let the Mouse go.

A little while later, the Lion was caught by hunters and tied up with strong ropes. Hearing the Lion's roar, the little Mouse ran to him and chewed through the ropes, setting the Lion free.

The Lion was amazed and learned that even small friends can do big things!

The Charcoal-Burner and the Fuller

Once upon a time, a Charcoal-Burner lived in his own house, making charcoal. One day, he met his friend, a Fuller, who cleaned and whitened clothes. The Charcoal-Burner asked the Fuller to come live with him so they could save money and be better neighbors. But the Fuller said, "I can't live with you, because every time I make something white, your charcoal dust will make it black again."

Moral: Sometimes, people's ways are too different to work together.

The Father and His Sons

A father had several sons who argued all the time. No matter what the father said, they kept fighting. One day, he asked them to bring him a bundle of sticks. He gave the bundle to each son and asked them to break it. No one could. Then, he took the sticks out one by one and asked them to break those. This time, they easily snapped the sticks.

The father said, "If you work together, you'll be strong like the bundle of sticks. But if you fight and stay apart, you'll be easily broken like these single sticks."

Moral: Unity makes us strong.

The Boy Hunting Locusts

A boy was catching locusts when he spotted a Scorpion. Thinking it was just another locust, he reached out to grab it. But the Scorpion showed its sharp stinger and said, "If you had touched me, you would have lost me and all your locusts!"

Moral: Be careful what you reach for.

The Cock and the Jewel

A rooster was scratching the ground, looking for food, when he found a shiny jewel. He looked at it and said, "If a person found you, they'd think you were very valuable. But I don't need jewels. I'd rather have a single grain of barley than all the jewels in the world."

Moral: What is valuable to one may not be valuable to another.

The Kingdom of the Lion

In the forest, the animals had a Lion as their king. The Lion was not mean or cruel, but kind and fair. One day, he called a meeting and told all the animals, both strong and weak, that they would now live together in peace. The Wolf and the Lamb, the Tiger and the Deer, and the Dog and the Rabbit would all be friends.

The Rabbit, feeling safe, said, "I've dreamed of this day when the weak can be with the strong without fear!" But right after saying that, the Rabbit ran away as fast as he could.

Moral: Old fears are hard to forget.

The Wolf and the Crane

A Wolf had a bone stuck in his throat and asked a Crane for help, offering a big reward. The Crane carefully put her head into the Wolf's mouth and pulled out the bone. Afterward, she asked for her reward, but the Wolf just grinned and said, "You should be happy that I let you take your head out of my mouth safely!"

Moral: If you help bad people, don't expect any thanks—be glad if you aren't hurt.

The Fisherman Piping

A Fisherman who loved music went to the shore with his flute and nets. Standing on a rock, he played beautiful tunes, hoping the fish would dance into his net on their own. But after waiting for a long time and seeing no fish, he put down his flute and cast his net into the water. When he pulled it up, it was full of fish! As they jumped around, the Fisherman said, "You wouldn't dance when I played music, but now you dance when I stop!"

Moral: Things don't always happen the way we expect them to.

Hercules and the Wagoner

A man was driving his wagon down a country road when it got stuck in the mud. He stood by the wagon, doing nothing except shouting for Hercules, the strong hero, to help him. Hercules appeared and said, "Why are you calling me? Push the wagon yourself and make your bullocks move. Don't ask for help until you've done everything you can first!"

Moral: The best help comes from helping yourself.

The Ants and the Grasshopper

One winter day, the Ants were busy drying the grain they had collected during the summer. A hungry Grasshopper, who had nothing to eat, came by and begged for some food. The Ants asked him, "Why didn't you store food during the summer?" The Grasshopper replied, "I was too busy singing all summer." The Ants laughed and said, "If you sang all summer, now you must dance to bed without supper this winter."

Moral: There's a time for work and a time for play—prepare for the future.

The Traveller and His Dog

A Traveller was getting ready for a journey and saw his Dog standing by the door, stretching. He said, "Why are you standing there? Everything is ready except you! Let's go!" The Dog wagged his tail and replied, "Master, I'm ready! It's you I've been waiting for."

Moral: Sometimes, those who are slow blame others for the delay.

The Dog and the Shadow

A Dog was crossing a bridge with a piece of meat in his mouth. As he looked down into the water, he saw his reflection and thought it was another Dog with a bigger piece of meat. Wanting the larger piece, he dropped his own to grab the one in the water. But when he snapped at the "other" Dog, the reflection disappeared, and his own meat was carried away by the stream.

Moral: Be happy with what you have, or you might end up with nothing.

The Mole and His Mother

A young Mole, who was blind since birth, once said to his Mother, "I'm sure I can see, Mother!" To test him, his Mother placed a few grains of frankincense in front of him and asked, "What is this?" The young Mole said, "It's a pebble." His Mother sighed and said, "My dear, I'm afraid you're not only blind, but you've lost your sense of smell too."

Moral: Don't pretend to have skills you don't actually possess.

The Herdsman and the Lost Bull

A Herdsman was looking after his flock in the forest when he lost a young Bull. He searched everywhere but couldn't find it. Frustrated, he promised that if he found out who had stolen it, he would offer a lamb to Hermes, Pan, and the forest gods. Soon after, he climbed a small hill and saw a Lion eating the Bull. Scared, he looked to the sky and said, "I promised a lamb if I found the thief, but now I'll offer a full-grown Bull if I can just get away safely!"

Moral: Be careful what you wish for—you might get more than you bargained for.

The Hare and the Tortoise

One day, a Hare made fun of a Tortoise for being so slow. The Tortoise laughed and said, "I may be slow, but I'll beat you in a race!" The Hare, thinking this was impossible, agreed to race. The Fox set the course and marked the finish line. When the race began, the Hare ran ahead and, thinking he had plenty of time, decided to take a nap. The Tortoise, however, kept going, slow and steady. When the Hare finally woke up and rushed to the finish, he found the Tortoise already there, resting after her steady journey.

Moral: Slow and steady wins the race.

The Pomegranate, Apple-Tree, and Bramble

A Pomegranate tree and an Apple tree were arguing over which of them was the most beautiful. As their argument grew louder, a Bramble bush nearby called out, "Stop fighting, my friends, and remember that no one is as impressive as I am!"

Moral: Those with little to boast about are often the loudest.

The Farmer and the Stork

A Farmer set nets in his field to catch Cranes that were eating his seeds. He trapped several Cranes, along with a Stork that had broken its leg in the net. The Stork begged for mercy, saying, "Please let me go, Farmer. I'm not like these Cranes. I have a good character, and I take care of my parents. Look at my feathers—they're not like a Crane's at all!" The Farmer laughed and said, "Maybe that's true, but I caught you with these Cranes, so you'll share their fate."

Moral: You are judged by the company you keep.

The Farmer and the Snake

One cold winter day, a Farmer found a Snake frozen and unable to move. Feeling sorry for the Snake, the Farmer picked it up and warmed it in his coat. The Snake, revived by the warmth, bit the Farmer and gave him a deadly wound. As the Farmer lay dying, he said, "I got what I deserved for showing kindness to a wicked creature."

Moral: Even the greatest kindness won't change the nature of the ungrateful.

The Fawn and His Mother

A young Fawn once asked his Mother, "You're bigger and faster than a dog, and you have sharp horns to defend yourself. Why are you so afraid of the hounds?" His Mother smiled and said, "You're right, my son, I do have all those advantages. But when I hear even one dog bark, I get so scared that I can't help but run away."

Moral: No amount of reasoning can give courage to someone who is naturally fearful.

The Bear and the Fox

A Bear was bragging about how kind he was, claiming that he respected humans so much he wouldn't even touch a dead body. A Fox, overhearing this, smiled and said, "It would be even better if you ate the dead and left the living alone!"

Moral: Actions speak louder than words.

The Swallow and the Crow

A Swallow and a Crow were arguing about whose feathers were better. The Swallow boasted about how beautiful her feathers looked in the spring. The Crow replied, "Your feathers may look nice in warm weather, but mine protect me through the cold winter."

Moral: Friends who are only around in good times aren't worth much.

The Mountain in Labour

One day, a Mountain made loud rumbling noises, and people from all over came to see what was happening. They expected something terrible to occur. After much anticipation, out popped a tiny Mouse!

Moral: Don't make a big fuss over nothing.

The Ass, the Fox, and the Lion

An Ass and a Fox teamed up to protect each other while hunting in the forest. Soon, they met a Lion. Fearing for his life, the Fox made a deal with the Lion, promising to help him capture the Ass if the Lion promised not to hurt him. The Fox then tricked the Ass into falling into a deep pit. Once the Ass was trapped, the Lion immediately turned on the Fox and attacked the Ass at his own leisure.

Moral: Betrayal often comes back to harm the betrayer.

The Tortoise and the Eagle

A Tortoise, basking in the sun, wished she could fly like the birds. Hearing her complaint, an Eagle asked what she would give in return if he helped her fly. The Tortoise promised all the riches of the Red Sea. The Eagle agreed, lifted her into the sky, but then dropped her from high up. The Tortoise crashed onto a mountain and died. With her last breath, she said, "I deserved this for wishing for something that was not meant for me."

Moral: If people got everything they wished for, it might lead to their downfall.

The Flies and the Honey-Pot

A group of Flies found an overturned jar of honey and started eating greedily. But as they fed, their feet got stuck in the sticky honey, and they couldn't fly or escape. As they were about to die, they said, "How foolish we were, all for a little bit of pleasure, we've ended up destroying ourselves."

Moral: Pleasure that comes with danger often leads to harm.

The Man and the Lion

A Man and a Lion were walking together and boasting about their strength. They came across a statue of a Man strangling a Lion. The Man proudly pointed to the statue, saying, "See how we humans are stronger than lions!" The Lion smiled and replied, "That statue was made by a human. If lions could make statues, it would show the Man under the Lion's paw."

Moral: Every story has two sides—what you see depends on who is telling it.

The Farmer and the Cranes

Once upon a time, some cheeky Cranes found a perfect spot to munch on some tasty wheat seeds that a Farmer had just planted. The Farmer spotted them and started swinging his sling in the air, making a big show of scaring them off. At first, the Cranes were frightened and flew away. But soon, they realized something. "Wait a minute," one Crane said, "he's not actually throwing anything!" So, they stopped caring about the Farmer's empty threats and kept on eating.

But the Farmer wasn't going to let his crops get destroyed so easily. "If they won't listen to my warnings," he thought, "it's time for real action!" He loaded his sling with stones and, with a swift shot, sent many Cranes flying for good. The rest of the Cranes quickly gathered and squawked, "Time to leave this place for good! This Farmer means business now!"

Moral: When warnings don't work, actions might have to follow.

The Dog in the Manger

In a cozy barn, a grumpy Dog found himself a comfy spot right in the middle of a pile of hay. Now, this hay wasn't meant for him—it was the delicious dinner for the hardworking Oxen. But every time one of the Oxen tried to come close to munch on the hay, the Dog would growl and snap at them, refusing to let anyone eat.

One of the Oxen sighed and said to his friend, "What a selfish Dog! He doesn't even like hay, but he won't let us eat it either."

Moral: Don't stop others from enjoying something just because you can't use it.

The Fox and the Goat

One hot day, a clever Fox accidentally fell into a deep well. Try as he might, he couldn't get out. Just as he was starting to lose hope, along came a thirsty Goat, looking for a drink. The Goat peered down into the well and asked, "Is the water good?"

The Fox, pretending everything was fine, grinned and said, "Oh, it's the best water you'll ever taste! Come on down, there's plenty for both of us!"

Without thinking twice, the Goat eagerly jumped into the well to quench his thirst. But as soon as he drank his fill, the Goat realized there was no way to climb back up. "Oh no," cried the Goat, "How will we get out?"

The Fox, who had been waiting for this moment, said, "I've got a plan! You stand still and press your front feet against the wall. I'll climb up your back and get out, and then I'll help you up too."

The Goat agreed, and the Fox quickly scrambled up the Goat's back and out of the well. But as soon as he was free, the Fox dashed off, leaving the Goat behind. "Hey! What about your promise?" called the Goat angrily...

The Fox turned back with a sly grin and said, "If you had thought before jumping in, you wouldn't be stuck! Next time, look before you leap."

Moral: Think ahead and make sure you have a way out before rushing into something.

The Bear and the Two travellers

Once upon a time, two friends were wandering through the woods, chatting and enjoying the day. Suddenly, out of nowhere, a big, growling Bear appeared right in front of them! The first friend, quick as a flash, climbed up a nearby tree and hid in the branches. But the second friend, who couldn't climb as fast, knew he had to think of something—fast! So, he dropped to the ground, held his breath, and pretended to be dead.

The Bear came closer, sniffing all around him. It even gave him a little nudge with its nose! But since the Bear thought he was dead, it eventually walked away, leaving him alone.

When the coast was clear, the friend in the tree climbed down and laughed, "What did the Bear say when it was whispering in your ear?"

The other friend got up and said, "Oh, it told me something very important: never travel with someone who runs away when danger comes!"

Moral: A true friend stands by you, even in tough times.

The Oxen and the Axle-Trees

One day, a heavy wagon loaded with goods was rolling down a bumpy country road, pulled by a pair of hardworking Oxen. The wagon's Axle-trees (the long bars connecting the wheels) began to creak and groan loudly with each bump, making quite a racket.

The Oxen turned their heads and said to the Axle-trees, "Hey! Why are you making so much noise? We're the ones pulling this heavy wagon and doing all the hard work. If anyone should be complaining, it's us!"

The Axle-trees were too busy creaking to reply, but the Oxen just shook their heads and kept moving forward, doing the work without a single groan.

Moral: Those who work the hardest often make the least fuss.

The Thirsty Pigeon

On a hot, sunny day, a Pigeon was flying around, feeling super thirsty. Then, up ahead, she spotted something wonderful—a goblet of water painted on a signboard! "Ah, finally, some water!" she thought, and with a flap of her wings, she zoomed toward it.

But, oh no! She didn't realize it was just a painting. She hit the signboard with a thud, and her wings got hurt. She fluttered to the ground in pain, only to be caught by a bystander who had seen the whole thing.

The Pigeon sighed, "If only I had been a bit more careful!"

Moral: Don't rush into things without thinking it through.

The Raven and the Swan

Once upon a time, a Raven saw a beautiful Swan gliding gracefully across a lake. The Swan's feathers were pure white, and the Raven was mesmerized. "I wish I had such beautiful feathers," the Raven thought, believing the Swan's color came from swimming in the water. Determined to change, the Raven left his usual home near the altars where he found food and moved to live by the lakes, hoping that bathing in the water would turn his feathers white too.

Day after day, the Raven washed himself in the cool lake, but no matter how much he bathed, his feathers remained black. And because he no longer had easy access to food, the poor Raven became weaker and weaker. Eventually, he realized his mistake—changing his surroundings didn't change who he truly was.

Moral: You can't change your true self by just changing your habits.

The Goat and the Goatherd

One sunny afternoon, a Goatherd was trying to gather his flock of goats. All of them returned except for one stubborn Goat, who wandered off on his own. The Goatherd whistled and called, but the Goat didn't listen. Frustrated, the Goatherd finally picked up a stone and threw it at the Goat, accidentally breaking its horn.

"Oh no," the Goatherd said, panicking. "Please don't tell my master! I didn't mean to hurt you."

The Goat, shaking its head, replied, "You don't have to worry about me telling him. My broken horn will say everything without me having to utter a word!"

Moral: Some things can't be hidden, no matter how hard you try.

The Miser

There once was a Miser who loved gold more than anything else in the world. He sold everything he owned and bought a big lump of gold, which he buried in a secret hole by an old wall. Every day, he visited the spot to admire his treasure, but he never used it for anything. One day, one of his workers noticed the Miser's strange habit of always visiting the same spot, so he secretly followed him. When the Miser left, the worker dug up the gold and stole it.

The next time the Miser came to gaze at his treasure, he found the hole empty. He was heartbroken and began wailing and pulling at his hair in despair. A neighbor, hearing his cries, came to see what was wrong. When the Miser told him what had happened, the neighbor said, "Why are you so upset? You never used the gold when you had it. You might as well go put a stone in the hole and imagine it's the gold—it will be just as useful to you!"

Moral: Wealth is useless if it's never put to use.

The Sick Lion

Once upon a time in a vast jungle, there lived a mighty Lion who was growing old and frail. Unable to hunt like he used to, the clever Lion came up with a sneaky plan to fill his belly. He returned to his cozy den and pretended to be very sick. News of the "sick Lion" spread quickly through the jungle, and many animals felt sorry for him. One by one, they came to visit him, bringing their sympathy—and themselves—right into his den!

The Lion enjoyed his tasty meals but soon became a little too full. However, one clever Fox noticed the pattern. When he came to visit, he stood just outside the cave, keeping his distance. "How are you feeling today, Mr. Lion?" asked the Fox.

"I'm doing quite okay, but why are you standing out there? Come in and chat!" replied the Lion, trying to coax the Fox inside.

"No, thank you," said the Fox, glancing around. "I see many paw prints going in, but none coming out!"

With that, the Fox wisely turned away, having learned that sometimes, it's best to be cautious and learn from the mistakes of others.

Moral: Be wise and heed the warnings of those who have suffered.

The Horse and the Groom

In a bustling farmyard, there lived a strong and beautiful Horse. His Groom loved to spend hours grooming and combing the Horse's shiny coat. However, this Groom had a secret: while he brushed and pampered the Horse, he also sneaked away the Horse's oats and sold them for his own profit!

One day, the Horse sighed and said, "Oh dear Groom, if you truly want me to be in great shape, it would be better to feed me more and groom me less!"

But the Groom, focused on his own selfish desires, didn't listen. The Horse knew that sometimes what looks like care may hide a sneaky trick!

Moral: True care involves providing what is truly needed, not just what looks nice.

The Ass and the Lapdog

On a lively little farm, there lived a hardworking Ass and a pampered Maltese Lapdog. The Ass toiled day in and day out, grinding corn and carrying heavy loads. The Lapdog, on the other hand, was adored by his master. He played tricks, received treats, and was always cuddled and kissed. The Ass couldn't help but feel envious.

"I wish I could be like that spoiled Lapdog, lounging around and getting treats!" thought the Ass. One day, in a fit of jealousy, he broke free from his halter and dashed into the house, trying to mimic the Lapdog's playful antics.

But chaos erupted! The Ass knocked over the table and sent dishes flying everywhere! The master's servants rushed in, shocked and alarmed, and quickly shooed the Ass back outside with loud shouts and swats.

As the poor Ass limped back to the stable, battered and bruised, he sighed, "Oh no! I've made a mess of everything! Why couldn't I be happy working with my friends instead of trying to be like that little Lapdog?"

Moral: Be content with who you are, and don't try to be someone you're not!

The Lioness

In a sunlit clearing of the great savannah, the animals were in a heated debate. They argued loudly about which creature could have the most babies at once. Excitedly, they gathered around the wise Lioness, hoping she would help settle their dispute.

"How many little ones do you have at a time?" they asked her curiously.

With a gentle smile, the Lioness replied, "I have just one little cub. But that cub is strong, brave, and will grow to be a magnificent Lion!"

The animals fell silent, realizing that it wasn't about having many babies, but rather having one exceptional one that truly mattered.

Moral: The value is in the worth, not in the number.

The Boasting Traveller

One sunny afternoon, a man returned from far-off lands, bubbling with excitement and stories. He bragged loudly about all the amazing adventures he'd had, from brave deeds to astonishing feats.

"I jumped so far in Rhodes that no one else could even come close!" he proclaimed, puffing out his chest. "And there are many witnesses to prove it!"

Just then, a smart onlooker interrupted, "If you really jumped that far, then you should have no trouble jumping for us right here! Show us!"

The boastful man paused; realizing that talking big was much easier than showing what he could do.

Moral: Actions speak louder than words.

The Cat and the Cock

Once upon a time, in a cozy barn, a crafty Cat caught a proud Cock. "Now, how can I enjoy my meal without looking like a villain?" thought the Cat.

"I'll tell you what," the Cat said slyly, "you're a noisy bird, keeping everyone awake with your crowing. You're a nuisance!"

The Cock flapped his wings, defending himself. "But I wake everyone up so they can start their day on time! I'm helping!"

"Ah, your excuses are very nice," purred the Cat with a sly grin, "but I'm still quite hungry!" And with that, the Cat devoured the Cock, ignoring his pleas.

Moral: Sometimes, the truth doesn't save you from a hungry villain.

The Piglet, the Sheep, and the Goat

In a small fold-yard, a Young Pig was enjoying his time with a Goat and a Sheep. One day, the shepherd came to grab the Piglet, and he squealed loudly in distress.

"Why do you cry so much?" asked the Sheep. "We let him handle us without making a fuss!"

The Piglet looked up and replied, "Oh dear friends, our situations are very different! When he grabs you, he only takes your wool or milk. But when he catches me, it's for my very life!"

The Sheep and Goat exchanged worried glances, finally understanding the Piglet's fear.

Moral: Everyone's troubles are different, and it's important to recognize them.

The Boy and the Filberts

One sunny afternoon, a curious boy spotted a pitcher brimming with delicious filberts. Unable to resist, he dipped his hand inside, grabbing as many as he could. But when he tried to pull his hand out, he found himself stuck!

"No, no! I can't lose these!" he wailed, tears rolling down his cheeks. Just then, a wise old man passing by said, "Why not take fewer? If you're satisfied with just a few filberts, you can easily pull your hand out!"

Realizing his mistake, the boy quickly let go of most of the nuts and pulled his hand free with a grin.

Moral: Sometimes, less is more!

The Lion in Love

In a dense forest, a mighty Lion fell in love with the beautiful daughter of a woodcutter. With a loud roar, he approached the woodcutter and asked for her hand in marriage. The woodcutter, frightened but clever, thought of a plan to avoid the Lion's request.

"I'll agree," said the woodcutter, "but only if you let me take out your teeth and claws. My daughter is afraid of them."

The Lion, eager to win her heart, agreed without hesitation. But when the toothless, clawless Lion returned to ask for the woodcutter's daughter, the woodcutter laughed and chased him away with a heavy club.

"Without your strength, you are no longer a threat," he said triumphantly.

Moral: Don't compromise your strength for love.

The Labourer and the Snake

Once upon a time, a snake made its home near a cozy cottage. One day, the snake bit the woodcutter's young son, leaving the father heartbroken. Furious and filled with grief, the father vowed to hunt down the snake.

The next day, as the snake slithered out for food, the woodcutter swung his axe but only managed to clip the end of the snake's tail! The snake hissed in pain and disappeared back into its hole.

Later, the woodcutter, fearing for his own safety, tried to make peace by leaving bread and salt at the snake's hole. The snake, still angry, replied, "There can be no peace between us. I'll always remember the loss of my tail when I see you, and you'll remember your son's death when you see me."

Moral: Injuries are hard to forget, especially from those who caused them.

The Wolf in Sheep's Clothing

Once upon a time, a clever Wolf was feeling very hungry. He thought, "If I can disguise myself, I can sneak into the sheep's pen and have a delicious meal!" So, he found a fluffy sheep's skin and put it on, looking just like one of the flock.

The Wolf trotted happily among the sheep, fooling the shepherd and blending in perfectly. That night, when the shepherd came to check on the sheep, he accidentally caught the Wolf instead of a sheep! Before the Wolf knew it, he was in trouble, and with one swift action, the shepherd took him out of the picture.

Moral: If you seek to deceive others, you may find yourself in danger!

The Ass and the Mule

One sunny day, a Muleteer set off on a journey, leading an Ass and a Mule, both loaded with heavy packs. As they traveled along the flat land, the Ass was able to carry his load without much trouble. But when they reached a steep mountain path, he began to struggle.

"Please, dear Mule," begged the Ass, "can you help me by taking a little of my load? I promise I'll carry the rest home!" But the Mule just shrugged and kept walking, ignoring the Ass's plea.

Soon, the Ass could bear the weight no longer and fell to the ground, too tired to go on. The Muleteer, not knowing what else to do, took the Ass's heavy load and piled it on the Mule. To top it off, he placed the skin of the Ass on the Mule, who groaned under the weight.

"Oh, if only I had helped my friend a little!" sighed the Mule. "Now I'm stuck with both his burden and him!"

Moral: Helping others in need can save you from greater trouble later!

The Frogs Asking for a King

Once upon a time, in a shimmering lake, the Frogs were feeling a bit sad. They had no ruler to lead them, and they decided they wanted a king! So, they sent some of their bravest ambassadors to Jupiter, the king of the gods, to ask for a leader.

Jupiter chuckled at their request and decided to play a little trick on them. He tossed a giant log into the lake with a big splash! The Frogs were terrified and dove deep into the water, hiding from the noise. But after a while, they noticed that the log wasn't moving at all. They slowly swam back to the surface and, feeling brave again, started climbing on top of the log, thinking it was a fine place to sit.

Soon, the Frogs grew bored and felt mistreated by having such a lazy king. So, they sent another group to Jupiter, asking for a new ruler. This time, he sent them a slippery Eel. At first, the Eel was nice, but the Frogs quickly realized he wasn't very strong or brave, either.

Frustrated, they sent yet another request to Jupiter for a different king. This time, he sent a Heron. But oh no! The Heron was very hungry and began to gobble up the Frogs one by one until there were none left to croak in the lake.

Moral: Sometimes, it's better to appreciate what you have than to keep asking for more!

The Boys and the Frogs

One sunny afternoon, a group of playful boys found a pond filled with Frogs. Excitedly, they began throwing stones at the Frogs, laughing as they watched them leap and splash. But one brave Frog popped his head above the water and shouted, "Please stop, boys! What's fun for you is really scary and deadly for us!"

The boys paused for a moment, surprised to hear the Frog speak. They didn't want to hurt anyone, and realizing their fun was causing harm, they decided to play a different game instead.

Moral: Always remember that your fun can affect others in ways you might not see!

The Sick Stag

In a peaceful meadow, a Sick Stag lay down to rest in a quiet corner, hoping to feel better soon. His friends, concerned for him, came to visit. They gathered around, but as they did, they each helped themselves to the delicious food meant for the Stag.

"Oh dear!" the Stag thought as he watched his food disappear. "I just wanted to rest and get better." But with all the visits, the Stag became weaker and weaker, and he soon realized he wasn't sick from illness but from losing his meals!

Moral: Sometimes, good intentions can bring more harm than help!

The Salt Merchant and His Ass

Once upon a time, a clever peddler set off to the seashore with his trusty Ass to buy some salt. After filling his sack, he began the journey home. As they crossed a stream, the Ass slipped and fell into the water. To the peddler's surprise, when the Ass stood up, the salt had melted away, making his load much lighter!

Delighted by this turn of events, the peddler returned to the seashore and filled his panniers with even more salt. But when they reached the stream again, the mischievous Ass decided to fall down on purpose this time, thinking he would lighten his load once more. As he rose, he brayed happily, but the peddler saw right through his trick.

Determined to teach the Ass a lesson, the peddler took him to the coast once more, but this time he bought sponges instead of salt. When they returned to the stream, the sly Ass once again pretended to slip and fell into the water. But oh no! The sponges soaked up the water and became heavy, doubling the weight on his back!

The Ass learned a valuable lesson that day: trying to trick others can lead to even bigger troubles for yourself!

The Oxen and the Butchers

In a peaceful meadow, a group of Oxen gathered to discuss a serious problem. They were tired of the Butchers, who were always taking them away for meat. "We should get rid of the Butchers!" one Ox declared, and the others cheered in agreement.

An old, wise Ox who had plowed many fields spoke up, "Wait a moment! While it's true the Butchers take us, they do it skillfully and without causing too much pain. If we get rid of them, we might end up in the hands of unskilled people who would hurt us even more."

The younger Oxen were confused. "But we can't just let them keep taking us away!" they protested.

The wise Ox replied, "No matter what happens, people will always want beef. If we remove the Butchers, we may suffer even worse fates."

The Oxen thought about this and realized that sometimes it's better to stick with what you know, even if it's not perfect, rather than risk something much worse!

Moral: Don't be too quick to trade one problem for another; it could be worse than the first!

The Lion, the Mouse, and the Fox

One sunny afternoon, a mighty Lion lay fast asleep in his cozy den, dreaming of all the adventures he would have when he woke up. But little did he know, a curious Mouse scampered across his mane and tickled his ears, waking him from his slumber!

Startled and angry, the Lion jumped up and searched high and low in his den for the tiny intruder. Just then, a clever Fox walked by and chuckled, "Look at you, oh great Lion! You're scared of a little Mouse?"

The Lion frowned and replied, "It's not the Mouse that frightens me; it's his boldness to wake me from my nap! Such rudeness cannot go unpunished!"

The Fox laughed and said, "Sometimes, little creatures can be more than they seem, but remember, not all liberties should be taken lightly."

Moral: Little offenses can lead to big reactions!

The Vain Jackdaw

Once upon a time, Jupiter, the king of the gods, decided to choose a king for all the birds. He announced that on a special day, every bird should come to him, and he would select the most beautiful one to rule over them.

A Jackdaw, who knew he wasn't the prettiest bird in the forest, had a clever idea. He scoured the woods and fields, gathering up colorful feathers that had fallen from his friends. He glued them onto his own feathers, transforming himself into a dazzling sight!

When the day arrived, all the birds gathered before Jupiter, each one eager to be chosen. The Jackdaw strutted forward, flaunting his new look, hoping to catch Jupiter's eye. But as Jupiter prepared to crown him king, the other birds recognized their own feathers and protested loudly, "This Jackdaw is not truly beautiful! He's just wearing our feathers!"

With a puff of wind, the birds plucked their feathers from the Jackdaw, leaving him with nothing but his own plain feathers.

Jupiter sighed and said, "True beauty comes from within, not from what you wear!"

Moral: Pretending to be someone you're not can lead to losing everything you had.

The Goatherd and the Wild Goats

Once upon a time, a friendly Goatherd was rounding up his goats at sunset when he stumbled upon a group of Wild Goats mingling with his flock. Thinking it would be a great idea to keep them safe for the night, he brought them all together in his fold.

The next day, a fierce snowstorm blew in, making it impossible for anyone to venture out. The Goatherd was worried about all his goats, so he made sure to give his own goats just enough food to survive, while he fed the Wild Goats extra treats, hoping they would like it so much that they would decide to stay with him forever.

When the snow melted, the Goatherd happily led all the goats out to graze, but to his dismay, the Wild Goats dashed away to the mountains, leaving him behind. Confused and upset, he shouted after them, "How could you be so ungrateful after all I did for you during the storm?"

One of the Wild Goats turned back and said, "We appreciate your kindness, but that's exactly why we're leaving! If you treated us better than your own goats, who's to say you wouldn't do the same to others who come after us?"

Moral: You should value your old friends because they are the ones who have always been there for you.

The Mischievous Dog

In a bustling town, there lived a playful little Dog who loved to sneak up on people and give them a little nip at their heels! It was all in good fun, but it made quite a few folks jump in surprise. His owner, wanting to teach him a lesson, decided to hang a little bell around his neck. "Now everyone will know when you're around!" he said.

The Dog, thinking this was a fancy accessory, strutted around the marketplace, ringing his bell proudly. He believed it made him the most distinguished dog in town!

One day, an old wise hound spotted him and shook his head. "Why do you prance about with that bell?" he asked. "It's not a badge of honor; it's a warning for everyone to steer clear of you. That bell lets them know you're the troublesome dog who bites!"

The little Dog was shocked. He had thought he was the star of the show, but now he realized the bell was a sign of his mischief, not of his fame.

Moral: Sometimes, being known for bad behavior is not the same as being famous.

The Fox Who Had Lost His Tail

Once upon a time, a clever Fox found himself caught in a trap. In his escape, he lost his bushy tail. Embarrassed and ashamed of his new appearance, he felt like an outcast among the other Foxes. Determined to change their opinions and make himself feel better, he hatched a plan.

Gathering a crowd of Foxes, he proposed a bold idea: "My fellow Foxes, you should all cut off your tails! Without them, you'll look much more attractive, and you'll feel lighter without that heavy brush dragging you down."

One Fox, wise to his scheme, raised a paw and interrupted, "If you hadn't lost your tail yourself, would you really be advising us to do the same?"

Moral: Often, those who are suffering want others to share their plight.

The Boy and the Nettles

There once was a young Boy who, while playing outside, accidentally touched a Nettle and got stung. In a hurry, he rushed home, crying, "Mom! I touched a Nettle and it hurts so much, but I was gentle with it!"

His Mother replied, "That's precisely why it stung you, dear. The next time you come across a Nettle, grasp it firmly, and it will be as soft as silk!"

Moral: Whatever you do, do it with determination and full effort.

The Man and His Two Sweethearts

In a quaint village, there lived a Middle-Aged Man who was courting two women at the same time. One was a youthful beauty, while the other was a dignified older lady. The elder, feeling uneasy about dating someone younger, would discreetly pull out his black hairs whenever he visited her. The younger lady, wanting to avoid being with an older man, did the same by yanking out his grey hairs.

Before long, the poor man found himself completely bald, caught in the middle of two women trying to change him to their liking.

Moral: Those who try to please everyone often end up pleasing no one at all.

The Astronomer

Once there was an Astronomer who spent his nights gazing at the stars, lost in the wonders of the cosmos. One evening, while deeply engrossed in his observations of the sky, he failed to notice the well in his path and fell straight into it. Injured and lamenting his misfortune, he cried out for help.

A neighbour, hearing his cries, rushed over and looked down into the well. With a bemused expression, he called out, "Old fellow, why do you look to the heavens while neglecting what's right in front of you?"

Moral: Keep your feet on the ground while you aim for the stars.

The Wolves and the Sheep

In a pasture, the Wolves approached the Sheep, expressing their grievances. "Why must there always be fear and slaughter between us?" they asked. "It is those troublesome Dogs that cause the trouble! They bark at us whenever we come near and attack us before we mean any harm. If you would only get rid of them, we could have peace."

The naïve Sheep, easily swayed by the Wolves' words, decided to dismiss the Dogs. But once the Dogs were gone, the Wolves seized the opportunity and attacked the unguarded flock at will.

Moral: Be wary of those who seek to deceive you; their intentions may not be as benign as they claim.

The Old Woman and the Physician

An old woman, having lost her sight, called for a physician to restore her vision. They struck a deal in front of witnesses: if he cured her blindness, she would pay him a sum of money; if not, she would owe him nothing.

The physician diligently visited her, applying his treatments but, unbeknownst to her, he was also stealing her possessions bit by bit. After taking all her belongings, he finally claimed to have healed her. When the old woman regained her sight, she found her home empty and refused to pay him.

The physician, infuriated, took her to court to demand payment. In her defense, the old woman said, "He speaks the truth about our agreement. He claims I am healed, but I still see nothing of my belongings. When I was blind, I saw my goods; now that he says I can see, I see nothing at all."

Moral: A clever argument can sometimes outwit the most cunning of deceivers.

The Fighting Cocks and the Eagle

Two game cocks were locked in a fierce battle for dominance over the farmyard. After a vigorous fight, one cock triumphed and sent the other fleeing. The victorious cock then flew up to a high wall, flapping his wings and crowing loudly in celebration of his victory.

However, while he reveled in his triumph, an eagle soaring overhead swooped down and carried him off in its talons. The vanquished cock, witnessing this, emerged from his hiding place and assumed control of the yard without opposition.

Moral: Pride often leads to one's downfall.

The Charger and the Miller

A charger, feeling the effects of old age, was sent to work in a mill instead of participating in battles. As he ground grain instead of charging into combat, he lamented his change in fortune, reminiscing about his glorious past. "Ah, Miller," he said, "I used to march into battle fully armored, groomed by a man, but now I find myself here grinding grain. I don't understand why I preferred this fate to the thrill of the battlefield."

The Miller replied, "Do not dwell on the past. It is the common lot of mortals to experience the ups and downs of fortune."

Moral: Life is filled with changes, and it's wise to accept them rather than mourn what has passed.

The Fox and the Monkey

Once, a monkey danced before a gathering of beasts, impressing them so much that they crowned him their king. Envious of his newfound power, a fox devised a plan to trick him. She discovered a piece of meat trapped in a snare and lured the monkey to it, claiming she had found a treasure that he should claim as his royal reward.

The monkey, driven by greed, approached the trap carelessly and was caught. Accusing the fox of betrayal, he cried, "You tricked me into this trap!" The fox retorted, "Oh, monkey, with your foolish mind, you think you are fit to be king over the beasts?"

Moral: A foolish ruler can easily be led astray by greed and naivety.

The Horse and His Rider

A horse soldier cared for his charger during the war, treating him as a partner and feeding him well with hay and corn. However, once the war was over, he neglected the horse, giving him only chaff to eat and making him carry heavy loads of wood, subjecting him to grueling labor.

When war was declared again, the soldier put on his horse's military gear and mounted, fully clad in heavy armor. The horse collapsed under the weight, saying, "You must now go to war on foot. You have turned me from a horse into an ass. How can you expect me to transform back in an instant?"

Moral: One cannot expect to benefit from something they have mistreated or neglected.

The Belly and the Members

The members of the body grew discontented with the belly, complaining, "Why should we work tirelessly to satisfy your needs when you do nothing but rest and indulge yourself?" In a fit of rebellion, they decided to cease providing for the belly. However, as time passed, the entire body weakened without nourishment, and the hands, feet, mouth, and eyes soon realized their mistake. They repented for their folly when they understood that the belly's well-being was essential for their own strength and survival.

Moral: Every part of a system has its role, and neglecting one can lead to the detriment of all.

The Vine and the Goat

During the vintage season, a vine was flourishing with abundant leaves and grapes. A goat happened by and began to nibble on the vine's tender tendrils and leaves. The vine complained, "Why do you harm me for no reason? Is there no grass for you to eat? You may think you can get away with this now, but soon enough, I shall have my revenge. If you cut me down to my roots, I will provide the wine to pour over you when you are sacrificed."

Moral: Harm done without cause may come back to haunt the wrongdoer.

Jupiter and the Monkey

Jupiter announced a contest among the beasts of the forest, promising a royal reward for the one whose offspring was deemed the most beautiful. The monkey, filled with maternal pride, presented her young—an ill-featured, flat-nosed, hairless little monkey. As the other animals laughed at her presentation, she proudly declared, "I do not know if Jupiter will reward my son, but I do know that in my eyes, he is the dearest and most beautiful of all."

Moral: A mother's love often blinds her to her child's flaws, and beauty is subjective.

The Widow and Her Little Maidens

A widow, who loved cleanliness, employed two young maidens to assist her with chores. Each morning, at the break of dawn, the widow would wake them at the crowing of a cock. Frustrated by the early rising and the hard work, the maidens decided to kill the cock to eliminate the source of their disturbance. However, once they executed their plan, they found that their mistress, no longer hearing the cock's call, began waking them even earlier, in the middle of the night, causing them even greater trouble.

Moral: Trying to eliminate a problem can sometimes lead to greater difficulties.

The Shepherd's Boy and the Wolf

A shepherd-boy, tasked with watching over a flock of sheep, entertained himself by falsely crying out, "Wolf! Wolf!" each time the villagers came to help, only to find it was a prank. The villagers grew weary of his antics and stopped responding. One day, when a real wolf appeared and began attacking the sheep, the boy cried out in genuine fear for help, but no one came to his aid. The wolf, unconcerned, then slaughtered the entire flock.

Moral: A liar will not be believed, even when telling the truth.

The Cat and the Birds

A cat, hearing that the birds in an aviary were unwell, disguised himself as a physician, carrying a cane and a bag of instruments. He knocked at the door and asked how they were, offering to prescribe a cure if they were ill. The birds replied, "We are all well and would like to stay that way, so please leave us alone."

Moral: Not everyone who appears to help has good intentions.

The Kid and the Wolf

A kid standing safely on the roof of a house spotted a wolf passing by and began to taunt and insult him from his high vantage point. The wolf looked up and replied, "You may mock me, but it is the roof beneath you that truly emboldens you."

Moral: Time and place often give the advantage to the weak over the strong.

The Ox and the Frog

An ox came to drink at a pool and accidentally stepped on a brood of young frogs, crushing one of them. When the mother frog noticed her missing child, she asked the remaining frogs what had happened. One of them explained, "A huge beast with four feet came and crushed him to death." The mother, trying to gauge the beast's size, began to puff herself up, asking if the beast was as big as her. Her son cautioned, "Stop trying to puff yourself up,

Mother; you would burst before you could ever match its size."

Moral: Know your limitations and don't attempt the impossible.

The Shepherd and the Wolf

A shepherd discovered a wolf's whelp and decided to raise it. He taught the wolf to steal lambs from nearby flocks. After some time, the wolf became proficient in thievery and said to the shepherd, "Since you have taught me how to steal, you should be careful, or you might lose some of your own flock."

Moral: Those who nurture and teach others must be wary of the consequences of their actions.

The Father and His Two Daughters

A man had two daughters: one was married to a gardener, and the other to a tile-maker. He first visited the gardener's wife, who expressed her contentment but wished for heavy rain to nourish the plants. Later, he visited the tile-maker's wife, who was also happy but desired dry weather so the bricks could dry properly. The father then remarked, "If your sister wishes for rain and you for dry weather, whose wish should I support?"

Moral: One cannot please everyone; sometimes desires conflict.

The Farmer and His Sons

As a father lay dying, he wanted to ensure that his sons would care for the family farm as he had. He told them there was a great treasure hidden in one of the vineyards. After his death, the sons dug up the entire vineyard in search of the treasure. They found nothing but, through their labor, reaped an extraordinary crop.

Moral: Hard work often yields rewards, even if the desired outcome is not realized.

The Crab and Its Mother

A crab mother asked her son why he walked sideways instead of straight. The young crab replied, "It's true, Mother, that walking straight is better. But if you can show me how to do it, I'll promise to follow." The mother crab tried but couldn't walk straight herself, thus acknowledging her child's point.

Moral: Example is more powerful than precept; one must practice what they preach.

The Heifer and the Ox

A heifer watched an ox laboring hard at the plow and mocked him for his misfortune. However, during the harvest festival, the owner released the ox from his yoke but bound the heifer with cords to take her to the altar for sacrifice. Seeing this, the ox smiled and said to the heifer, "This is why you were allowed to live in idleness, so you could be sacrificed."

Moral: Idleness may lead to unforeseen consequences.

The Swallow, the Serpent, and the Court of Justice

A swallow returning from abroad built a nest in the wall of a Court of Justice, where she hatched seven young birds. A serpent passing by ate the fledglings. Grieving over her loss, the swallow lamented, "Woe is me, a stranger! In a place where justice prevails, I alone suffer wrong."

Moral: Even in places that seem safe, injustice can still occur.

The Thief and His Mother

A boy stole a lesson book from a classmate and brought it home. His mother not only refrained from punishing him but encouraged his actions. He then stole a cloak and received the same commendation. As he grew, his thefts escalated until he was caught and led to execution. His mother, filled with sorrow, followed the crowd and beat her breast. The son asked to speak to her and bit off her ear instead. When she scolded him for his cruelty, he replied, "If you had punished me for my first theft, I wouldn't have ended up like this."

Moral: Early discipline is essential to prevent future wrongdoing.

The Old Man and Death

An old man was chopping wood in the forest. After a long day, he grew weary and sat down by the roadside, asking for Death to come to him. Death appeared and asked why he had summoned him. The old man quickly replied, "I wish you would help me lift this load back onto my shoulders."

Moral: In times of weariness, we often seek escape from our burdens only to find ourselves wanting the strength to bear them again.

The Fir-Tree and the Bramble

A fir-tree boasted to a bramble, "You are of no use at all while I am sought after for roofs and houses." The bramble replied, "You should remember the axes and saws that are coming to cut you down. You might find it better to be a bramble than a fir-tree."

Moral: Better to have modest circumstances without danger than to be wealthy and in constant peril.

The Mouse, the Frog, and the Hawk

A mouse who lived on land became friends with a frog that resided in the water. One day, the frog, up to mischief, tied the mouse's foot to his own and led him to the meadow for food. Gradually, he pulled the mouse toward the pool, then jumped in, dragging the mouse along. The mouse struggled and drowned, and his body floated to the surface tied to the frog. A hawk spotted the mouse and swooped down, taking both the mouse and the frog, which was also eaten.

Moral: Those who harm others may find themselves harmed in return.

The Man Bitten by a Dog

A man who had been bitten by a dog sought someone to heal him. A friend advised him, "If you want to be cured, take a piece of bread, dip it in the blood from your wound, and give it to the dog that bit you." The man laughed at this suggestion, saying, "If I do that, it would be like inviting every dog in town to bite me."

Moral: Offering kindness to those who mean you harm only empowers them to hurt you further.

The Two Pots

A river carried two pots downstream—one made of earthenware and the other of brass. The earthen pot warned, "Please stay away; if you touch me even slightly, I'll break. I have no desire to come near you."

Moral: Friendship is best found among equals.

The Wolf and the Sheep

A wounded wolf lay in his den, calling to a passing sheep to fetch him water from a nearby stream. "If you bring me drink, I will provide myself with meat," he promised. The sheep replied, "If I bring you water, you'll surely make me provide the meat as well."

Moral: Deceptive intentions can be easily discerned.

The Aethiop

A man who bought a black servant believed his dark skin was due to dirt from his previous masters. After bringing him home, he subjected the servant to endless scrubbing, hoping to clean him. Despite his efforts, the servant remained unchanged and caught a severe cold.

Moral: Some traits are inherent and cannot be altered by superficial means.

The Fisherman and His Nets

A fisherman, skilled in his trade, cast his net successfully and captured a large haul of fish. He expertly managed to keep all the big fish but could not prevent the smaller ones from slipping through the net's meshes and falling back into the sea.

The Huntsman and the Fisherman

A huntsman returning from the field encountered a fisherman carrying a basket full of fish. The huntsman desired the fish, while the fisherman longed for the game in the huntsman's bag. They agreed to trade their catches and were both pleased with the exchange, continuing this practice for some time. However, a neighbor warned them, "If you continue this way, you will soon lose the pleasure of your exchanges, and you will each wish to keep the fruits of your own labor."

Moral: Sometimes, moderation enhances enjoyment.

The Old Woman and the Wine-Jar

An old woman discovered an empty wine jar that had once contained fine old wine. Although it was empty, it still had a delightful fragrance. She greedily held it to her nose multiple times and remarked, "How delicious this must have been! The sweet scent is proof of the fine wine that once filled it."

Moral: The memory of a good deed or experience lingers on, even after the moment has passed.

The Fox and the Crow

A crow stole a piece of meat and sat in a tree, holding it in her beak. A fox, eager to get the meat for himself, devised a clever plan. He exclaimed, "Oh, how beautiful the crow is in her shape and complexion! If only her voice matched her beauty, she would truly be the Queen of Birds!" This flattery worked, as the crow wanted to prove her voice was just as lovely. She cawed loudly, causing the meat to fall from her beak. The fox quickly snatched it up and said, "Dear crow, your voice is fine, but your wits are lacking."

Moral: Flattery can lead to foolish actions.

The Two Dogs

A man owned two dogs: a hound trained for hunting and a housedog that guarded the home. After a successful hunting trip, the man always gave a large share of the spoils to the housedog. The hound, feeling resentful, complained, "It's unfair that I do all the work while you feast on the results of my efforts!" The housedog replied, "Don't blame me; blame our master for not training me to work. I depend on your labor for my meals."

Moral: Children should not be held accountable for their parents' choices or actions.

The Stag in the Ox-Stall

A stag, pursued by hounds and blinded by fear, sought refuge in a farmyard, hiding among the oxen in a shed. An ox warned him, "Why would you willingly put yourself in danger by hiding in the house of your enemy?" The stag replied, "Please let me stay here, and I will find a way to escape."

As evening came, the herdsman approached to feed his cattle but did not see the stag. Even the bailiff and laborers passed through the shed without noticing him. The stag felt relieved and thanked the oxen for their help. However, one ox cautioned him, "We wish you well, but you're still in danger. There is one more to come, and he has many eyes."

Just then, the master entered, complaining about the lack of fodder and the uncleanliness of the stall. As he inspected the area, he spotted the stag's antlers peeking out from the straw. He quickly summoned his laborers and ordered them to seize the stag and kill him.

Moral: Seeking refuge in dangerous places can lead to greater peril.

The Hawk, the Kite, and the Pigeons

The pigeons, frightened by a kite, sought help from a hawk to protect them. The hawk quickly agreed to assist, and when they allowed him into their cote, they discovered he caused more destruction and killed more of them in one day than the kite could catch in an entire year.

Moral: Avoid a remedy that is worse than the disease.

The Widow and the Sheep

A poor widow had just one sheep. When it was time to shear, she decided to save money by shearing him herself. However, she used the shears so poorly that she ended up cutting the sheep's flesh along with the fleece. In pain, the sheep lamented, "Why do you hurt me, Mistress? What good does my blood do for the wool? If you want my fleece, the shearer can do it without hurting me; but if you want my flesh, go to the butcher who will kill me immediately."

Moral: The least outlay is not always the greatest gain.

The Wild Ass and the Lion

A wild ass and a lion formed an alliance to capture forest animals more easily. The lion provided strength, while the wild ass contributed speed. After successfully hunting, the lion decided to divide the prey into three parts. He declared, "I'll take the first share because I am king; the second share as your partner; and the third share—you will hand it over to me quickly, or you'll regret it."

Moral: Might makes right.

The Eagle and the Arrow

An eagle perched high on a rock was watching a hare, eager to catch it as prey. An archer, hiding nearby, took aim and struck the eagle with an arrow. Mortally wounded, the eagle glanced at the arrow and noticed that its feathers were from his own wings. With a sorrowful exclamation, he lamented, "It is a double grief to me that I should perish by an arrow feathered from my own wings."

Moral: We often contribute to our own downfall.

The Sick Kite

A kite, nearing death, implored his mother, "O Mother! Do not mourn for me, but invoke the gods for my life to be prolonged." His mother replied, "Alas! Which god do you think will pity you? Is there any deity whom you have not offended by stealing parts of their sacrifices from their altars?"

Moral: We must make friends in prosperity if we would have their help in adversity.

The Lion and the Dolphin

A lion walking along the shore spotted a dolphin rising from the waves and suggested they form an alliance, as both were rulers in their realms—the king of beasts on land and the sovereign of the sea. The dolphin agreed. Later, when the lion fought a wild bull, he called for the dolphin's help. Although the dolphin wanted to assist, he couldn't reach the land. The lion accused him of treachery. The dolphin replied, "Do not blame me, my friend, but Nature, which has granted me sovereignty over the sea but denied me the ability to live on land."

Moral: One should not blame others for their limitations set by nature.

The Lion and the Boar

On a hot summer day, a lion and a boar arrived simultaneously at a small well to drink. They began to argue fiercely over who should drink first, which quickly escalated into a deadly fight. In the midst of their struggle, they paused to catch their breath and noticed vultures waiting nearby, eager to feast on whichever one fell first.

Realizing the danger they faced from the vultures, they made peace, saying, "It is better for us to make friends than to become the food of crows or vultures."

Moral: Unity is strength; internal conflict can lead to mutual destruction.

The One-Eyed Doe

A doe, blind in one eye, grazed close to the edge of a cliff, hoping to stay safe from predators. She turned her good eye toward the land to spot any hunters or hounds approaching, while her blind eye was turned toward the sea, where she expected no danger. However, some boatmen sailing by spotted her and took a shot, mortally wounding her. As she lay dying, she lamented, "O wretched creature that I am! To be so cautious of land dangers, only to find the seashore I sought for safety to be far more perilous."

Moral: Sometimes the very precautions we take can lead us into greater danger.

The Shepherd and the Sea

A shepherd, watching over his sheep near the calm shore, became eager to venture into commerce. He sold all his flock to invest in a cargo of dates and set sail. A violent storm soon struck, threatening to sink his ship. In desperation, he threw all his goods overboard and barely escaped with his life. Later, when he saw the calm sea again, he remarked, "It is again in want of dates, and therefore looks quiet."

Moral: The calm before the storm can be deceptive; appearances can be misleading.

The Ass, the Cock, and the Lion

An ass and a cock shared a straw yard when a hungry lion approached. The lion was about to pounce on the ass when the cock, known for having a peculiar aversion in the lion, crowed loudly. Startled, the lion fled. Encouraged by the lion's fear, the ass attempted to chase him down. However, after running a short distance, the lion turned around, seized the ass, and tore him to pieces.

Moral: False confidence can lead to perilous situations.

The Mice and the Weasels

The Weasels and the Mice were engaged in an ongoing war, with much bloodshed. The Weasels were almost always victorious. The Mice, believing that their repeated defeats were due to the lack of leadership and discipline, decided to elect leaders from among their ranks. They chose the most renowned Mice, known for their family descent, strength, wisdom, and courage. To distinguish themselves as leaders, these generals adorned their heads with straws, making them easily identifiable during the battle. When the war was once again declared, the Mice were promptly defeated. While most of the Mice escaped to their holes, the generals, because of the straws on their heads, were unable to fit into the holes and were captured and eaten by the Weasels.

Moral: The more one seeks honor, the greater the danger one faces.

The Mice in Council

Once upon a time, a group of Mice decided to hold a meeting to figure out how to stay safe from their big enemy, the Cat. They talked about many ideas, and the best one they could think of was to tie a little bell around the Cat's neck. That way, when the Cat came near, they could hear the bell ringing and scamper back to their holes!

But when they started to decide who would be brave enough to tie the bell on the Cat, they realized nobody wanted to do it! Everyone was too scared. So, in the end, the Mice learned that it's easier to come up with a plan than to actually carry it out!

The Wolf and the Housedog

One sunny day, a hungry Wolf met a big, fluffy Mastiff wearing a wooden collar around his neck. The Wolf was curious and asked, "Who feeds you so well while you have to wear that heavy thing?"

The Mastiff replied proudly, "My master takes care of me."

The Wolf shook his head and said, "Oh no! I would never want to be in your place. That collar looks too heavy and would make me lose my appetite!"

And so, the Wolf learned that sometimes, having everything you need isn't worth it if it comes with too many rules!

The Rivers and the Sea

One day, the Rivers gathered together to talk to the big Sea. "Why do you change us from sweet and fresh water into salty water when we flow into you?" they asked.

The Sea, with a twinkle in its waves, replied, "If you don't want to become salty, then just stop flowing into me!"

The Rivers realized that they needed to be careful about where they went. Sometimes, it's better to stay true to yourself than to mix with others who might change you!

The Playful Ass

One curious Ass climbed up onto the roof of a barn and started jumping around, having lots of fun! But soon, he accidentally broke some tiles. The barn owner saw this and hurried up to chase him down, giving the Ass a little smack with a stick.

The Ass complained, "But wait! I saw the Monkey doing the same thing yesterday, and everyone laughed!"

The barn owner chuckled and said, "Well, you're not a Monkey! Every animal has its own way of having fun. Just be careful next time!"

And from that day on, the Ass learned that having fun is great, but it's also important to think about the consequences!

The Three Tradesmen

Once upon a time, in a great city, the people were worried because their home was surrounded by enemies. They gathered together to discuss how to protect their city.

First, a Bricklayer stood up and said, "We should use bricks! They're strong and will make a great wall!"

Next, a Carpenter chimed in, "No, no! Timber is much better! It can build a sturdy defense!"

Then, a Currier joined the conversation, saying, "I think we should use hides! Leather is tough and can protect us!"

The three tradesmen argued about which material was the best, but they couldn't agree. Finally, the townsfolk realized that everyone had their own ideas about how to help. They learned that sometimes, when there are different opinions, it's important to listen to everyone and work together!

The Master and His Dogs

One stormy day, a man was stuck in his country house. To feed himself, he first had to kill his sheep, then his goats, and finally, when the storm continued, he slaughtered his oxen.

Watching all this, the Dogs of the house gathered together. One said, "We better leave! If our master is using his animals for food, he won't think twice about getting rid of us!"

They realized that if their master couldn't take care of his own animals, he wouldn't take care of them either. The Dogs decided it was time to find a new home where they would be treated better. This taught them that a kind friend looks after all his family, even the furry ones!

The Wolf and the Shepherds

One sunny day, a Wolf walked by and spotted some Shepherds happily enjoying a big meal of mutton. The Wolf felt a bit jealous and said, "If I were to eat like you, you would be very upset!"

The Shepherds looked at him and said, "Of course! That wouldn't be fair at all! But we work hard for our food, and you don't!"

The Wolf realized that it was easy to complain about others, but the Shepherds worked for what they had. He learned that it's important to earn your meals and respect others who do the same!

The Dolphins, the Whales, and the Sprat

In the deep blue ocean, there was a fierce battle between the Dolphins and the Whales. They were arguing and splashing all around.

A little Sprat popped his head out of the water and said, "Hey, I can help! Let me be the judge and help you make peace!"

One of the Dolphins laughed and said, "We would rather fight each other than let you decide anything! You're too small!"

The Sprat realized that even though he wanted to help, sometimes, others might not want to listen to someone who seems small. He swam away, knowing that everyone has to find their own way to resolve their issues. It's important to be kind and understanding, even when things get tough!

The Ass Carrying the Image

One day, an Ass was asked to carry a beautiful wooden statue through the busy streets of a city. As he walked along, the people saw the statue and bowed down to it, showing their respect. The Ass thought they were bowing to him, feeling very proud of himself. He stood tall, puffed up with pride, and refused to move any further.

Seeing this, the driver gave the Ass a gentle nudge with his whip and said, "Oh, silly Ass! They are not bowing to you! They respect the statue, not you!"

The Ass learned that it's not wise to take credit for something that isn't his. It's important to remember that respect should go to those who deserve it, not to oneself!

The Two Travellers and the Axe

Two friends were walking together on a path when one of them spotted an axe lying on the ground. "I found an axe!" he exclaimed happily.

"No, no!" said the other friend. "We found it together! Let's say 'we.'"

They didn't walk very far before they noticed the owner of the axe running towards them. The first friend gasped, "We're in trouble!"

"Nay," replied the other with a grin. "Let's stick to what we said before. Say 'I' since you were so quick to claim it before!"

They both laughed, realizing that when you share the good things, you should also share the trouble. It's fair to take responsibility together!

The Old Lion

Once upon a time, there was an old Lion who was tired and sick. He lay down, feeling very weak. One day, a Boar came along and bumped into him, taking revenge for something the Lion had done long ago. Soon after, a Bull charged at the Lion, acting as if he were his enemy.

Finally, an Ass, seeing that others were being brave, decided to kick the Lion in the forehead. The old Lion sighed and said, "I can handle the brave animals who dare to face me, but being treated like this by you, a silly creature, is truly a shame!"

The Lion's words reminded everyone that sometimes, it's not just about being brave; it's about being respectful, too!

The Old Hound

There was once a strong Hound who, in his younger days, could chase down any animal in the forest. But now, as he grew old, he was still trying his best. One day, he spotted a Boar and tried to catch him. The Hound grabbed the Boar's ear, but his old teeth couldn't hold on, and the Boar got away.

When his master arrived, he was very disappointed and scolded the Hound. The Hound looked up and said, "Please don't be upset with me, dear master! My heart is still strong, but my body is old. I deserve to be praised for the good dog I used to be, not blamed for my age!"

The Hound's words taught everyone that as we grow older, it's important to remember the good things we've done, even if we can't do everything we used to!

The Bee and Jupiter

Once upon a time, a busy Bee from Mount Hymettus decided to take some sweet honey to Jupiter, the king of the gods, as a special gift. Jupiter loved the honey so much that he promised the Bee she could ask for anything she wanted.

The Bee thought for a moment and said, "Please, give me a sting so I can protect my honey from anyone who tries to take it!"

Jupiter frowned a little because he cared for people and didn't want them to be hurt. But he had promised to grant her wish, so he said, "You can have your sting, but be careful! If you use it, you will lose it, and that could be very dangerous for you."

The Bee realized that her wish could cause her trouble, and she learned that sometimes, wanting to hurt others can lead to our own problems.

The Milk-Woman and Her Pail

One sunny day, a Farmer's daughter was happily carrying a Pail of milk back home. As she walked, she started dreaming about what she could do with the money she would make from selling the milk. "With that money, I could buy three hundred eggs! Those eggs will hatch into two hundred fifty chickens! Then I can sell the chickens at a great price and buy myself a beautiful new dress for the Christmas parties!"

As she imagined all the fun she would have, she got so excited that she tossed her head back. Suddenly, her milk pail slipped from her hands and spilled all over the ground! All her dreams about the dress and the parties disappeared in an instant.

The girl learned a valuable lesson: sometimes, it's best to focus on what's happening right now instead of getting lost in dreams.

The Seaside Travellers

A group of Travelers was walking along a beautiful seashore when they spotted something far away on the water. "Look! A big ship!" one traveler exclaimed. They climbed up a tall cliff to get a better look, eagerly waiting to see the ship come into the harbor.

As the object got closer, the wind blew it toward the shore, and they soon realized it was just a small boat—not a ship at all! When it finally reached the beach, they discovered it was only a pile of sticks tied together. One traveler sighed and said, "What a disappointment! We waited for nothing!"

They all chuckled at their excitement over something that turned out to be just wood. They learned that sometimes what we hope for isn't as great as it seems!

The Brazier and His Dog

In a cozy little workshop, there lived a Brazier and his beloved little Dog. The Dog loved to nap while his master worked hard hammering metals. But whenever the Brazier sat down to eat, the Dog would wake up and wag his tail, hoping for a tasty treat.

One day, the Brazier pretended to be angry and said, "Oh, you lazy little Dog! While I work, you snooze on the mat, and when I eat, you suddenly want food! Don't you know that we must work to enjoy the good things in life?"

The little Dog listened and realized that hard work is important. He promised to help his master more, so they could both enjoy their meals together!

The Ass and His Shadow

One hot day, a Traveller hired an Ass to take him to a faraway place. When they stopped to rest, the Traveller wanted to get out of the scorching sun and sought shade under the Ass. However, the Ass's owner also wanted to share the cool shade!

The Traveller insisted, "I paid for the Ass, so I should have the shade too!" The owner argued back, "But I only rented you the Ass, not his shadow!"

As they began to argue and push each other, the Ass decided he'd had enough. He galloped away, leaving them both in the sun!

The Traveller and the owner learned that sometimes, when we argue about little things, we can lose what really matters.

The Ass and His Masters

Once there was an Ass who worked for an herb-seller. The herb-seller didn't give him enough food and made him work too hard. One day, the tired Ass went to Jupiter, the king of the gods, and asked to be given a new master.

Jupiter warned him, "You might regret this choice, but I will help you." He sold the Ass to a tile-maker. Soon, the Ass realized he had to carry even heavier loads! So, he went back to Jupiter and begged for another master.

This time, Jupiter sold him to a tanner. The Ass was scared and groaned, "Oh no! Now my hide will be used to make leather after I'm gone! It would have been better to stay with my first master, even if he didn't treat me well."

The Ass learned that sometimes, it's better to appreciate what you have rather than keep asking for something better.

The Oak and the Reeds

One day, a huge Oak tree was uprooted by a powerful wind and fell across a stream. It saw some tiny Reeds nearby and said, "How can you little things survive these strong winds? You must be so weak!"

The Reeds replied, "We bend and sway with the wind, while you stand tall and fight against it. That's why you were knocked down, and we are still here!"

The Oak learned that sometimes, it's better to be flexible and go with the flow than to be rigid and strong.

The Fisherman and the Little Fish

A Fisherman who depended on his catch had a busy day and caught a tiny little Fish. The little Fish, struggling to breathe, begged for his life, "Please don't eat me! I'm so small and not worth much. If you let me go, I promise to grow big and become a delicious catch for you later!"

The Fisherman smiled and said, "It would be silly of me to let go of a sure meal for the chance of a bigger fish that may never come. I need to eat today!"

The little Fish learned that sometimes it's important to appreciate what you have instead of hoping for something better in the future.

The Hunter and the Woodman

Once, a not-so-brave Hunter was looking for signs of a Lion in the forest. He met a Woodman chopping down trees and asked, "Have you seen any Lion tracks or know where he lives?"

The Woodman replied with a grin, "I can show you the Lion right now!"

The Hunter turned pale, his teeth chattering in fear. "No, thank you! I just want to see where he walked, not the Lion himself!"

This taught the Hunter that true bravery means not just talking tough but also being brave in action.

The Wild Boar and the Fox

One sunny day, a Wild Boar was rubbing his tusks against a tree. A curious Fox strolled by and asked, "Why are you sharpening your teeth? There's no danger around!"

The Boar replied wisely, "I'm getting ready! It's best to sharpen my tusks now rather than when I really need them in a fight."

The Boar's advice reminds us that it's good to be prepared before trouble comes.

The Lion in the Farmyard

One day, a Lion wandered into a Farmer's yard. The Farmer, trying to catch him, quickly shut the gate. Trapped, the Lion got angry and started chasing the sheep, then the oxen! The Farmer, realizing he was in trouble, opened the gate to let the Lion escape.

After the Lion left, the Farmer lamented the loss of his sheep and oxen. His wife, watching everything, said, "You brought this on yourself! How could you think it was safe to keep a Lion in your yard when you tremble at his roar from far away?"

This story teaches us that we should be careful and think things through before making decisions.

Mercury and the Sculptor

Once, Mercury wanted to find out what people thought of him. He disguised himself as a man and visited a Sculptor's studio. After looking at some statues, he asked the Sculptor how much he would sell the statues of Jupiter and Juno for.

The Sculptor told him the prices. Mercury then pointed to a statue of himself and said, "You should charge a lot more for this one! It's the statue of the Messenger of the Gods, after all!"

The Sculptor chuckled and said, "If you want the other statues, I'll throw this one in for free!"

This shows that sometimes people don't recognize the true value of things, even when they're right in front of them.

The Swan and the Goose

Once, a wealthy man bought a Goose for his dinner and a beautiful Swan for its lovely songs. One night, when it was dark, the cook went to catch the Goose for dinner. But in the darkness, he accidentally grabbed the Swan instead!

As the cook threatened to cook him, the Swan started singing a beautiful melody. His lovely voice made the cook realize his mistake, and he let the Swan go free.

This story shows that sometimes our special talents can save us from trouble!

The Swollen Fox

One day, a very hungry Fox found some leftover bread and meat hidden in the hollow of a big oak tree. He couldn't resist the tasty treat and crept inside to enjoy a big feast. But after eating so much, he got so full that he couldn't squeeze back out!

As he groaned and complained about his situation, another Fox walked by and heard him. Curious, he asked, "Why are you so sad?"

The hungry Fox explained what happened. The wise Fox chuckled and said, "You'll have to wait until you're as slim as you were when you came in. Then you'll be able to escape!"

This story teaches us that overindulgence can lead to trouble, and sometimes we have to be patient to find a way out.

The Fox and the Woodcutter

One day, a Fox was running away from some hunting dogs when he stumbled upon a Woodcutter chopping down a tree. The Fox, frightened and looking for a safe place to hide, asked the Woodcutter for help.

"Please, can you hide me in your hut?" asked the Fox.

The Woodcutter agreed, and the Fox quickly slipped inside, hiding in a cozy corner. Soon, the huntsman and his hounds came searching for the Fox. The Woodcutter saw them approaching and, while he was talking to the huntsman, he kept pointing towards his hut!

But the huntsman didn't notice the Woodcutter's hints and moved on in search of the Fox. Once the coast was clear, the Fox slipped out of the hut. The Woodcutter called after him, "Hey! You ungrateful Fox! I saved your life, and you didn't even thank me!"

The Fox replied, "I would have thanked you if your words matched your actions. You pointed to the hut while pretending not to see me!"

This story reminds us that actions speak louder than words, and we should always be sincere!

The Birdcatcher, the Partridge, and the Cock

Once, a Birdcatcher was getting ready to enjoy a simple dinner when a friend unexpectedly dropped by. Unfortunately, he hadn't caught any birds and had to kill his special decoy, a pied Partridge. The Partridge begged for its life, saying, "If you let me live, I can help you catch more birds in the future! Who will call to you and sing you to sleep?"

The Birdcatcher thought about it and decided to spare the Partridge. But then he turned to the Cock, who was just starting to crow, and said, "I might have to use you for dinner instead!"

The Cock pleaded, "Wait! If you kill me, who will wake you up at dawn? Who will let you know when it's time to check your nets?"

The Birdcatcher agreed, "You're right! You're great at waking me up, but my friend and I are still very hungry."

This story teaches us that sometimes, when we're really in need, we may have to make tough choices.

The Monkey and the Fishermen

One day, a curious Monkey watched some Fishermen casting their nets into a river. He was fascinated and wanted to try it himself. After the Fishermen left for lunch, the Monkey climbed down from the tree and picked up a net. He thought, "How hard can this be?"

But as he threw the net into the water, he got all tangled up! Before he knew it, he was in over his head and couldn't escape. As he struggled, he realized, "I shouldn't have tried to catch fish when I've never even used a net before!"

This story reminds us that we should stick to what we know and not try to do things that are beyond our experience!

The Flea and the Wrestler

One day, a tiny Flea landed on the foot of a powerful Wrestler. The Flea bit him, and the Wrestler cried out for help from Hercules, the strongest hero of all.

But when the Flea jumped back on his foot again, the Wrestler sighed, "O Hercules! If you can't help me with this little Flea, how can I expect you to help me against bigger challenges?"

This story teaches us that sometimes we face small problems that can feel just as overwhelming as the big ones!

The Two Frogs

Once upon a time, two Frogs lived happily in a cozy pool. But when the summer heat dried up their home, they decided to look for a new place to live. As they hopped along, they spotted a deep well filled with water. One Frog excitedly said, "Let's jump in! This well has plenty of water and will be a great place for us to stay!"

The other Frog, however, was more cautious. "But what if the water runs out? How will we climb back out of this deep well?"

This story teaches us that it's important to think ahead and consider the consequences of our decisions before jumping into something new!

The Cat and the Mice

In a certain house, a sneaky Cat discovered that it was filled with Mice! Excitedly, the Cat sneaked in and began to catch them one by one. The Mice were terrified and hid in their little holes, making it hard for the Cat to catch them.

Realizing she needed to trick the Mice out, the clever Cat jumped onto a peg and pretended to be dead, hoping they would come out. But one brave Mouse peeked out and said, "Oh no, dear Cat! Even if you pretend to be a meal-bag, we won't fall for your trick!"

This story reminds us to be clever and cautious, especially when we suspect someone is trying to trick us!

The Lion, the Bear, and the Fox

One sunny day, a powerful Lion and a strong Bear both spotted a tasty Kid at the same time. They fought fiercely for it, scratching and biting each other until they were both exhausted and lay on the ground, tired and worn out.

A clever Fox watched from a distance. Seeing the two big animals too weak to move, the Fox dashed in, grabbed the Kid, and scampered away as fast as his little legs could carry him. The Lion and the Bear, seeing the Fox escape with their prize, groaned, "Oh no! We fought so hard, and now a Fox gets to enjoy the fruit of our labor!"

This story teaches us that sometimes one person does all the hard work while someone else reaps the rewards!

The Doe and the Lion

One day, a frightened Doe was being chased by hunters. In her panic, she spotted a cave and quickly ran inside to hide. Little did she know, the cave belonged to a fierce Lion!

The Lion saw her come in and decided to wait quietly. Once the Doe thought she was safe, the Lion jumped out and attacked her. The Doe cried out, "Oh no! I escaped from the hunters, only to end up in the jaws of a wild beast!"

This story teaches us that while trying to avoid one danger, we should be careful not to fall into another.

The Farmer and the Fox

A Farmer was really upset with a Fox for stealing his chickens. One day, he finally caught the tricky Fox and wanted to get back at him. So, he tied a long rope soaked in oil to the Fox's tail and set it on fire!

In a panic, the Fox ran straight into the Farmer's fields filled with wheat, causing chaos everywhere. But sadly, the Farmer was left with nothing to harvest that year and returned home feeling very sad.

This story reminds us that seeking revenge can sometimes lead to more trouble for ourselves than for the one we want to punish.

The Seagull and the Kite

A hungry Seagull tried to eat a fish that was way too big for him. Unfortunately, it got stuck in his throat, and he couldn't fly. He lay on the shore, feeling very weak and sad.

A Kite flew by and saw the poor Seagull. "You brought this on yourself," said the Kite. "A bird like you shouldn't be looking for food in the sea!"

This story teaches us that everyone should stick to what they know best and mind their own business!

The Philosopher, the Ants, and Mercury

One day, a Philosopher stood by the shore and watched a ship sink. He was very upset and complained about how unfair it was that so many innocent people drowned just because of one bad person on the ship.

While he was thinking about this, a tiny Ant climbed up and stung him. Angered, the Philosopher stomped on the Ants nearby, squashing many of them. Suddenly, Mercury appeared and said, "How can you judge what is fair when you just treated these little Ants so badly?"

This story teaches us that we should be careful about judging others when we might do the same thing ourselves.

The Mouse and the Bull

One day, a tiny Mouse bit a big Bull on the leg. The Bull was very angry and tried to catch the Mouse, but the Mouse quickly escaped into his hole. The Bull tried to dig him out but got tired and fell asleep outside the hole.

When the Bull woke up, the Mouse peeked out and bit him again before scurrying back into safety. The Bull was confused and frustrated, and the Mouse said, "Just because you're big doesn't mean you can always win. Sometimes, the small can cause a lot of trouble too!"

This story reminds us that size doesn't determine strength or power.

The Lion and the Hare

One day, a Lion found a Hare sleeping peacefully. Just as he was about to grab her for lunch, a young Hart came by, and the Lion decided to chase after the Hart instead. The Hare woke up and ran away quickly.

After a long chase, the Lion couldn't catch the Hart and returned to find the Hare had escaped too. He sighed and said, "I should have been happy with the meal I had instead of chasing after something bigger!"

This story teaches us to appreciate what we have instead of always wanting more.

The Peasant and the Eagle

A Peasant found an Eagle trapped in a snare. He admired the beautiful bird and set it free. The grateful Eagle, seeing the Peasant resting under a weak wall, flew down and snatched a bundle from his head. When the Peasant ran after the Eagle, it dropped the bundle.

When the Peasant returned, he found that the wall had collapsed! He realized that the Eagle had saved his life by warning him.

This story teaches us that acts of kindness can come back to help us in unexpected ways.

The Image of Mercury and the Carpenter

There was a very poor Carpenter who had a wooden statue of Mercury. Every day, he prayed to the statue to make him rich, but instead, he got poorer. Frustrated, he took the statue down and smashed it against the wall. To his surprise, gold coins spilled out from the statue!

The Carpenter was confused and said, "You don't help me when I treat you kindly, but when I'm angry, I'm rewarded!"

This story shows that sometimes we don't understand how things really work until something surprising happens.

The Bull and the Goat

One day, a Bull was running away from a Lion and hid in a cave. Inside, a Goat attacked him with his horns. The Bull calmly said, "Go ahead and butt me; I'm not afraid of you. I fear the Lion. If he goes away, I'll show you who is stronger!"

This story teaches us that it's wrong to take advantage of someone when they're in trouble.

The Dancing Monkeys

A Prince had some Monkeys that he trained to dance. They wore fancy clothes and performed beautifully, making everyone clap. One day, a mischievous courtier threw nuts onto the stage. The Monkeys forgot about dancing and fought over the nuts, tearing off their costumes. The audience laughed, and the show ended in chaos.

This story reminds us that distractions can lead us away from what we should be doing.

The Fox and the Leopard

The Fox and the Leopard argued about who was more beautiful. The Leopard showed off his pretty spots, but the Fox interrupted and said, "You may have spots, but I'm more beautiful in my mind!"

This story teaches us that true beauty comes from within.

The Monkeys and Their Mother

A Monkey had two babies. She loved one and cared for it a lot but ignored the other. Sadly, the baby she loved too much was smothered by her hugs, while the neglected one grew strong despite being ignored.

This story shows that good intentions don't always lead to good outcomes.

The Oaks and Jupiter

The Oaks complained to Jupiter, saying, "We are always in danger of being cut down!" Jupiter replied, "You only have yourselves to blame because your strong wood is very useful to people. If you weren't so valuable, they wouldn't chop you down so often!"

This story teaches us that sometimes our strengths can lead to our troubles.

The Hare and the Hound

A Hound chased a Hare but gave up after a long run. A goat-herd saw this and teased the Hound, saying, "The little Hare runs faster than you!" The Hound replied, "You don't understand. I was running for dinner, but he was running for his life!"

This story reminds us that sometimes we fight harder for things that really matter to us.

The Traveller and Fortune

A tired Traveller lay down near a deep well to rest. Just as he was about to fall in, Fortune appeared and woke him up. She said, "Please be careful! If you fall in, everyone will blame me, even though it's your fault for not being careful."

This story teaches us that we are responsible for our own actions and their consequences.

The Bald Knight

A Bald Knight, who wore a wig, went out hunting. Suddenly, a gust of wind blew off his hat and wig, making everyone laugh. The Bald Knight stopped his horse and joined in the laughter, saying, "Isn't it funny that hair that isn't mine can fly away when it has left the man it belongs to?"

This story reminds us that it's good to laugh at ourselves and not take things too seriously.

The Shepherd and the Dog

One night, a Shepherd was putting his sheep into their fold when he almost closed the door on a wolf. The Dog, noticing the wolf, barked, "Master, how can you keep the sheep safe if you let a wolf in with them?"

This story teaches us that we should be careful about who or what we allow into our lives, as some can be harmful.

The Lamp

One day, a Lamp that was burning too brightly boasted that it shone brighter than the sun. Suddenly, a strong wind blew, and the Lamp was put out. Its owner lit it again and said, "Stop boasting! Just be happy to shine quietly. Even the stars don't need to be lit again."

This story teaches us to be humble and not boast about our strengths.

The Lion, the Fox, and the Ass

A Lion, a Fox, and an Ass decided to help each other catch food. After a successful hunt, the Lion asked the Ass to divide the food into three parts. The Ass did his best and gave the Lion and Fox the first choice. Angered, the Lion ate the Ass. Then, the Lion asked the Fox to divide the food. The Fox quickly gathered all the food into one big pile and left himself the smallest piece. The Lion praised him, saying, "Who taught you to divide like that?" The Fox replied, "I learned from the Ass, by watching what happened to him."

This story teaches us to learn from the mistakes of others.

The Bull, the Lioness, and the Wild-Boar Hunter

One day, a Bull found a lion's sleeping cub and gored it with his horns. The Lioness was heartbroken when she discovered her cub was dead. A Wild-Boar Hunter, watching from a distance, said to her, "Think about all the parents who have lost their children because of you."

This story reminds us that our actions can have consequences for others.

The Oak and the Woodcutters

A Woodcutter cut down a tall Oak tree and used branches from the Oak to make wedges to split the trunk. The Oak sighed and said, "I can handle the axe cutting my roots, but it hurts me to be chopped up using my own branches."

This story teaches us that misfortunes caused by ourselves are the hardest to bear.

The Hen and the Golden Eggs

A farmer and his wife had a Hen that laid a golden egg every day. They thought the Hen must have a treasure inside, so they decided to kill it to get all the gold at once. But when they opened it, they found it was just like any other Hen. By trying to get rich quickly, they lost the daily gold they had.

This story teaches us to be grateful for what we have and not to be greedy.

The Ass and the Frogs

One day, an Ass was carrying a load of wood and stumbled while crossing a pond. He fell into the water and groaned because he couldn't get up with the heavy load. Some Frogs nearby heard him and said, "What would you do if you had to live here all the time? You're just complaining about a little fall!"

This story teaches us that we should be grateful for what we have and not complain about small troubles.

The Crow and the Raven

A Crow was jealous of a Raven because the Raven was seen as a bird that brought good luck. One day, when some travelers were passing by, the Crow flew up into a tree and cawed loudly to get their attention. The travelers wondered what it meant until one said, "Let's keep going; it's just a Crow, and her caw isn't a sign of anything important."

This story teaches us that pretending to be something we're not only makes us look foolish.

The Trees and the Axe

A man entered a forest and asked the Trees for a handle for his axe. The Trees agreed and gave him a young ash-tree. After making the axe handle, the man started chopping down the biggest trees in the forest. An old oak tree sadly said to a nearby cedar, "We shouldn't have given up the ash; now we've lost everything."

This story reminds us that giving up something small can lead to losing something much greater.

The Crab and the Fox

A Crab left the sea to search for food in a green meadow. Unfortunately, a hungry Fox found the Crab and ate him. Before being eaten, the Crab said, "I deserve this because I shouldn't have left the sea where I belong."

This story teaches us to be content with who we are and where we belong.

The Woman and Her Hen

A woman had a Hen that laid one egg every day. Wanting more, she decided to feed the Hen extra food to get two eggs. The Hen became fat but stopped laying eggs altogether.

This story teaches us that greed can lead to losing what we already have.

The Ass and the Old Shepherd

One day, a Shepherd was watching his Ass when suddenly he heard cries from enemies nearby. He urged the

Ass to run with him to escape, but the Ass replied lazily, "Why should I run? I'm just a pack animal, and it doesn't matter to me who I serve as long as I carry the load."

This story reminds us that often, the poor suffer the same regardless of who is in charge.

The Kites and the Swans

Once, Kites and Swans could sing beautifully. But one day, they heard a horse neighing and became fascinated by it. They tried to imitate the sound, but in their efforts, they forgot how to sing.

This story teaches us that wanting things that seem better can cause us to lose what we already have.

The Wolves and the Sheepdogs

The Wolves approached the Sheepdogs and said, "Why don't you join us? You are like us in many ways, but you serve humans who mistreat you. If you come with us, we will share the sheep and live freely!" The Sheepdogs were tempted and followed the Wolves into their den, but the Wolves attacked and killed them.

This story reminds us to be careful who we trust; not everyone has our best interests at heart.

The Hares and the Foxes

The Hares were in trouble and needed help fighting the Eagles. They asked the Foxes to join them. The Foxes replied, "We would love to help, but we know who you are and who you're up against."

This story teaches us to think carefully before getting involved in a conflict.

The Bowman and the Lion

A very skilled Bowman went into the mountains to hunt. All the animals ran away from him except for a Lion, who decided to challenge him. The Bowman shot an arrow at the Lion and said, "This is what you can expect from me!" The

Lion was scared and ran off. A Fox, who saw everything, told the Lion not to be afraid, but the Lion replied, "If he sends such a dangerous arrow, I can't imagine how powerful he is in person!"

This story warns us to be cautious of people who can attack from a distance.

The Camel

When people first saw the Camel, they were scared of its large size and ran away. But after a while, they noticed how gentle and calm the Camel was and started to approach it. Eventually, they realized it was a friendly animal and even let children drive it.

This story teaches us that getting used to something can help us overcome our fears.

The Wasp and the Snake

A Wasp decided to sit on a Snake's head and sting him repeatedly until the Snake was in great pain. Unable to get rid of the Wasp, the Snake put his head under a heavy wagon wheel and said, "At least we can perish together."

This story shows us how powerful enemies can push us to the edge, but we should be careful not to let them lead us to our downfall.

The Dog and the Hare

A Hound chased a Hare, sometimes trying to bite her and sometimes pretending to play. The Hare said, "I wish you would be honest with me. If you are my friend, why do you hurt me? If you are my enemy, why do you act friendly?"

This story teaches us that true friends are honest and shouldn't act in ways that confuse us.

The Bull and the Calf

A Bull was trying hard to squeeze through a narrow path to reach his stall. A young Calf came up and offered to show him the way. The Bull replied, "Thanks, but I've known this path long before you were born!"

This story reminds us that experience often teaches us more than what others can offer.

The Stag, the Wolf, and the Sheep

A Stag asked a Sheep to lend him some wheat and said that the Wolf would guarantee it. The Sheep was suspicious and replied, "The Wolf takes what he wants and runs away, and you are too fast for me. How will I find you when it's time to pay back?"

This story teaches us that trusting the wrong friends can lead to trouble.

The Peacock and the Crane

One day, a Peacock spread its beautiful feathers and laughed at a Crane, saying, "Look at my colourful plumage! I look like a king, while you are dull and grey." The Crane replied, "That may be true, but I can fly high in the sky and sing to the stars, while you strut around on the ground like a chicken."

This story teaches us that looks aren't everything; true worth comes from what we can do.

The Fox and the Hedgehog

A Fox was swept away by a river and ended up in a deep ravine, where he was too hurt to move. Hungry flies landed on him, making him uncomfortable. A Hedgehog passing by asked, "Do you want me to chase the flies away?" The Fox replied, "No, don't! The flies already fed on me and don't sting too much. If you scare them off, hungrier ones will come and take all my blood!"

This story shows us that sometimes it's better to deal with a smaller problem than to risk a bigger one.

The Eagle, the Cat, and the Wild Sow

An Eagle built her nest high in a tall oak tree. A Cat found a cozy spot in the trunk, while a Wild Sow made a home at the base with her piglets. The Cat wanted to take advantage of the situation, so she went to the Eagle and said, "The Sow wants to knock down the tree and eat your babies!" Then, she went to the Sow and warned, "The Eagle is going to swoop down and take your little pigs!"

Both the Eagle and the Sow became too scared to leave their homes. Eventually, they both starved while the clever Cat went out to hunt for food, getting fat while her neighbors perished.

This story teaches us that those who sow discord and fear can gain the most from the misfortune of others.

The Thief and the Innkeeper

A Thief rented a room at an inn, hoping to steal something to pay for his stay. After a few days without luck, he noticed the Innkeeper wearing a new coat. The Thief sat down beside him and pretended to be in distress. He yawned and howled like a wolf, alarming the Innkeeper.

"Why are you howling?" the Innkeeper asked.

The Thief replied, "When I yawn three times, I turn into a wolf and attack people! Please hold my clothes while I deal with this." As he yawned again, the Innkeeper, scared, tried to run away. The Thief grabbed his coat and said, "Don't leave! Hold my clothes or I'll go wild!" After a third yawn and howl, the Innkeeper, terrified, dropped the coat and ran inside the inn.

The Thief took off with the coat and never returned.

This story teaches us that not every tale is true and that we should be careful about who we trust.

The Mule

A Mule, full of energy from too much food and not enough work, bragged to himself, "I must be the child of a fast racehorse!" The next day, after a long journey, he grew tired and realized, "Maybe my father was just a donkey after all."

This story reminds us that we should know our limits and not overestimate ourselves.

The Hart and the Vine

A Hart (a type of deer), being chased by hunters, hid under the big leaves of a Vine. The hunters passed by without noticing him. Feeling safe, the Hart started nibbling on the Vine's leaves. But then one hunter noticed the movement and shot an arrow, hitting the Hart.

As he lay dying, the Hart said, "I deserve this because I shouldn't have harmed the Vine that saved me."

This story teaches us to be grateful for those who help us and not to take advantage of their kindness.

The Serpent and the Eagle

A Serpent and an Eagle were fighting. The Serpent was about to win when a countryman saw them. He helped the Eagle escape from the Serpent's grip. Angry that he lost his meal, the Serpent put poison in the countryman's drinking horn.

Just as the countryman was about to drink, the Eagle noticed and quickly struck the man's hand, grabbing the horn and carrying it away to safety.

This story teaches us that good deeds can lead to protection, and it's important to be aware of dangers around us.

The Crow and the Pitcher

A thirsty Crow saw a pitcher and flew to it, hoping for water. When he arrived, he found that the water was too low for him to reach. He tried everything but couldn't get the water. Finally, he had an idea! He picked up stones and dropped them into the pitcher one by one. Slowly, the water rose high enough for him to drink.

This story shows that when we face problems, we can find creative solutions.

The Two Frogs

Two Frogs were neighbours. One lived in a deep pond, safe and hidden, while the other lived in a shallow gully along a busy road. The Frog in the pond warned the other to move to safety, but the gully Frog refused, saying he was used to his home.

One day, a heavy wagon passed through the gully and crushed the gully Frog.

This story teaches us that stubbornness can lead to trouble, and it's wise to listen to advice that keeps us safe.

The Wolf and the Fox

Once, a big and strong Wolf was born among wolves. Because of his size, the other wolves called him "Lion." The Wolf thought they were serious, so he left his wolf friends to hang out with lions instead.

An old Fox, seeing this, said, "I hope I never make a fool of myself like you! You might be big among wolves, but in a group of lions, you're still just a wolf."

This story reminds us that pride can lead to foolishness and that we should know our place.

The Walnut Tree

A Walnut Tree stood by the roadside and grew many nuts. However, people passing by hurt the tree by throwing stones and sticks to get the nuts. The Walnut Tree cried out, "Oh, how sad it is! The very people I help with my nuts hurt me in return!"

This story teaches us that sometimes, the ones we help might not appreciate our kindness.

The Gnat and the Lion

A Gnat bragged to a Lion, saying, "I'm not afraid of you! You may be big and strong, but I can defeat you!" The Gnat flew around the Lion, stinging him on the face. The Lion tried to catch the Gnat but only hurt himself in the process. The Gnat flew away, boasting of his victory.

But soon after, the Gnat got caught in a spider's web and was eaten. He lamented, "Oh no! I can defeat the strongest animals, yet I was caught by this tiny spider!"

This story reminds us that even the smallest creature can bring downfall, and one should not underestimate others.

The Monkey and the Dolphin

A sailor took a Monkey on a long voyage for company. During the trip, a big storm sank the ship, and everyone had to swim to safety. A Dolphin saw the Monkey struggling and thought it was a man, so he helped him onto his back to take him to shore.

As they neared land, the Dolphin asked, "Are you from Athens?" The Monkey proudly replied that he was from a noble family there. When asked about the famous harbor, the Monkey said he knew it well and claimed it was a good friend.

The Dolphin became angry at the Monkey's lies, so he dunked him underwater and drowned him.

This story teaches us that lying can lead to trouble and that it's best to be honest about who we are.

The Jackdaw and the Doves

A Jackdaw saw some Doves living in a cozy place filled with food. Wanting to join them, he painted himself white to look like a Dove. At first, the Doves welcomed him, thinking he was one of them, especially since he stayed quiet.

But one day, the Jackdaw forgot to be silent and started chattering. The Doves quickly realized he wasn't one of them and chased him away. The Jackdaw then tried to return to the other Jackdaws, but they didn't recognize him because of his new colour and kicked him out too.

In the end, the Jackdaw wanted to be part of two groups but ended up belonging to neither.

This story teaches us that pretending to be someone you're not can lead to losing your true friends.

The Horse and the Stag

Once, a Horse enjoyed the wide-open field all by himself until a Stag came and shared the pasture. Angry, the Horse wanted revenge on the Stag, so he asked a man for help. The man said he would help if the Horse would let him ride on his back.

The Horse agreed, thinking he would get his revenge. However, instead of punishing the Stag, he ended up working for the man and lost his freedom.

This story reminds us that seeking revenge can sometimes lead to our own downfall.

The Kid and the Wolf

A Kid was out in the pasture all alone when a Wolf started chasing him. Realizing he couldn't escape, the Kid said to the Wolf, "I know I'm going to be your dinner, but before that, can you play me a tune to dance to?"

The Wolf agreed and began to play music while the Kid danced. But soon, the sounds attracted some hounds, who came running to chase the Wolf away. The Wolf turned to the Kid and said, "This is what I get for trying to entertain you when I'm supposed to be the hunter!"

This story teaches us that sometimes, trying to please others can lead to unexpected trouble.

The Prophet

One day, a wizard was in the marketplace, telling fortunes to people passing by. Suddenly, someone rushed up to him and said that a thief had broken into his house and was stealing his belongings. The wizard sighed and ran off quickly to save his things.

A neighbour saw him running and called out, "Hey! You can predict everyone else's future, but why didn't you see this coming for yourself?"

This story reminds us that even those who claim to know everything can sometimes overlook their own problems.

The Fox and the Monkey

A Fox and a Monkey were walking together when they came across a cemetery filled with tombstones. The Monkey pointed to the stones and said, "All of these monuments are for my ancestors, who were important and respected people in their time."

The Fox replied, "That's a clever lie! But how do you know they can't come back to tell the truth about it?"

This story teaches us that telling false stories can be risky, especially when there's no one to confirm them.

The Thief and the Housedog

One night, a Thief decided to break into a house. To keep the Housedog quiet and prevent it from barking, he brought some slices of meat to feed the dog. As the Thief threw the meat, the Dog said, "You think giving me food will silence me? I'll be even more alert now! Your sudden kindness seems suspicious. I'll watch closely to make sure you aren't trying to hurt my master."

This story teaches us to be cautious of those who show sudden kindness, as they might have hidden motives.

The Man, the Horse, the Ox, and the Dog

One cold day, a Horse, an Ox, and a Dog were all seeking shelter from the harsh weather. A kind Man welcomed them into his home, lit a fire, and provided food for each of them. The Horse enjoyed the oats, the Ox had plenty of hay, and the Dog was fed meat from the Man's own table.

Feeling grateful for the Man's kindness, the animals decided to give him something in return. They agreed to share his life by dividing it into three parts and giving each part their own special traits.

The Horse took the first part of his life, so in youth, people can be impulsive and stubborn. The Ox chose the second part, so that in middle age, people work hard and focus on saving money. Finally, the Dog took the last part of the Man's life, making older people often grumpy, hard to please, and protective of their home.

This story teaches us that our experiences and traits can shape who we are at different stages of life.

The Apes and the Two Travellers

Two men, one who always told the truth and the other who only told lies, travelled to a land ruled by Apes. The King of the Apes wanted to know what people thought of him, so he ordered the two men to come before him. He gathered all the Apes around him and set up a throne, just like a human king.

When the Lying Traveller was asked how the King seemed to him, he flattered him, saying he was a mighty king. The King, pleased with the lie, rewarded him with a gift.

Then, the truthful Traveller was asked the same question. He replied honestly, saying the King was just a good Ape and that his friends were also good Apes. The King became angry at this truth and punished the truthful Traveller.

This story shows that sometimes, telling the truth can have consequences, especially when dealing with those who prefer flattery.

The Wolf and the Shepherd

A Wolf followed a flock of sheep for a long time without attacking any of them. The Shepherd was cautious at first and watched the Wolf closely, thinking he was a danger. But over time, the Shepherd started to see the Wolf as a protector of the sheep instead of a threat.

One day, the Shepherd had to leave the flock to go to the city and thought it was safe to leave the Wolf in charge. But when the Shepherd returned, he found most of his sheep gone because the Wolf had taken the opportunity to eat them.

The Shepherd then realized, "I shouldn't have trusted a Wolf to look after my sheep!"

This story teaches us that sometimes, it's not wise to trust those who have a reputation for being dangerous.

The Hares and the Lions

The Hares gathered together to discuss equality, insisting that everyone should be treated the same. The Lions, who were much stronger, listened to the Hares and said, "Your ideas sound nice, but you lack the strength we have."

This fable reminds us that having good ideas is one thing, but being able to enforce them requires strength and power.

The Lark and Her Young Ones

A Lark built her nest in a wheat field during spring. One day, as the young Larks were almost ready to fly, the farmer said he would ask his neighbours to help him harvest the wheat. One young Lark heard this and worried about where they should move for safety.

The mother Lark replied, "Don't worry yet. The farmer who only asks friends for help isn't serious." A few days later, the farmer said he would come himself with labourers to harvest the wheat.

When the mother Lark heard this, she told her young ones, "It's time to leave! The farmer is serious now; he won't trust anyone else but himself to do the work."

This story teaches us that relying on yourself is often the best way to ensure your safety.

The Fox and the Lion

Once, a Fox who had never seen a Lion came across one in the forest. He was so scared that he almost fainted! The next time he saw the Lion, he was still frightened, but not as much as before. By the third time, the Fox felt brave enough to walk up and chat with the Lion.

This story teaches us that getting to know someone can help reduce our fears and prejudices.

The Weasel and the Mice

An old Weasel, unable to catch mice like he used to, decided to roll in flour and pretend to be food. Several Mice jumped on him, thinking he was a treat, and were caught and killed. One wise old Mouse watched from a distance and said, "You will get what you deserve for pretending to be something you're not!"

This fable reminds us that deception can lead to dire consequences.

The Boy Bathing

A Boy was swimming in a river when he suddenly found himself in danger of drowning. He called out for help to a traveler passing by. Instead of helping him, the traveler scolded the boy for being reckless. The boy shouted back, "Please help me first, and you can scold me later!"

This teaches us that advice without action is not helpful when someone is in danger.

The Ass and the Wolf

One day, an Ass saw a Wolf coming to catch him. To escape, he pretended to be hurt and asked the Wolf to help him by pulling out a thorn from his foot. The Wolf, wanting to eat the Ass, agreed and focused on finding the thorn. Just then, the Ass kicked the Wolf with his hind legs and ran away.

The Wolf, now hurt, said, "I deserve this for trying to be a healer instead of sticking to what I know best!"

This story teaches us that we should stick to our own skills and not overreach into areas we don't understand.

The Seller of Images

There was a man who made a wooden statue of Mercury and tried to sell it. No one wanted to buy it, so he started shouting that it was a statue of a great benefactor who could bring wealth. A bystander asked, "If he's so great, why are you selling him? You could enjoy his gifts yourself!" The man replied, "I need help right now, but he gives his gifts very slowly."

This fable teaches us that sometimes people sell things they don't really believe in.

The Fox and the Grapes

One hungry Fox saw some delicious black grapes hanging from a vine. She tried everything to reach them but couldn't get to them no matter what. Finally, she walked away and said, "Those grapes are probably sour anyway!"

This story shows that when we can't have something, we often say we didn't want it in the first place.

The Man and His Wife

A man had a wife who was disliked by everyone in his household. Curious if she was disliked by her family too, he sent her to visit her father. When she returned, he asked how her visit went. She said the herdsmen and shepherds looked at her with dislike. The man replied, "If they disliked you, imagine how those who see you every day feel!"

This teaches us that small signs can reveal the bigger truth.

The Peacock and Juno

The Peacock complained to Juno, the goddess, saying that while the nightingale had a beautiful song, he was laughed at when he tried to sing. Juno comforted him, saying, "You are much more beautiful and large. Your feathers are like a dazzling rainbow!" The Peacock replied, "But what is beauty if I can't sing?" Juno explained, "Everyone has their own special gifts: you have beauty, the eagle has strength, the nightingale has song, and so on. Each one should be happy with what they have."

This story teaches us to appreciate our own unique talents instead of envying others.

The Hawk and the Nightingale

A Nightingale was singing happily on an oak tree when a hungry Hawk swooped down and caught him. The Nightingale begged the Hawk to let him go, saying he was too small to fill the Hawk's belly and that he should chase larger birds instead. The Hawk replied, "Why would I let go of an easy meal right in front of me to look for something bigger that I can't even see?"

This fable teaches us that sometimes, it's wise to take the opportunity in front of us rather than chase after something uncertain.

The Dog, the Cock, and the Fox

A Dog and a Cock were good friends and decided to travel together. They found a place to sleep in a thick wood. The Cock flew up to a tree branch while the Dog settled in a hollow trunk below. In the morning, the Cock crowed loudly, and a hungry Fox heard him. The Fox wanted to eat the Cock and pretended to be friendly, saying he wanted to meet the Cock. The clever Cock asked the Fox to wake the Dog below to let him in. When the Fox went down, the Dog jumped out and caught him, tearing him apart.

This story shows that cleverness can help us escape danger.

The Wolf and the Goat

A Wolf saw a Goat on a steep cliff and wanted to eat her, but he couldn't reach her. He called out to the Goat, pretending to care for her safety, and said she should come down to avoid falling. He told her there were delicious meadows where he stood. The Goat replied, "You're not inviting me for the grass, but because you want to eat me!"

This fable reminds us to be cautious of those who may have bad intentions.

The Lion and the Bull

A Lion wanted to catch a Bull but was scared to attack him because he was so big. So, the Lion decided to trick the Bull. He approached the Bull and said he had killed a fine sheep and invited the Bull to eat with him. The Lion hoped that while the Bull was distracted, he could attack him. When the Bull came to the Lion's den, he saw no sheep but noticed the big cooking pots and spits. He realized it was a trap and said, "I'm leaving because I see no sign of a sheep, but I see plenty of ways you plan to eat a Bull!"

This teaches us to be observant and trust our instincts when something seems off.

The Goat and the Ass

A man had a Goat and an Ass. The Goat envied the Ass because he had more food and said, "You work too hard, grinding grain and carrying heavy loads. You should pretend to be sick and fall into a ditch so you can rest." The Ass listened to the Goat and fell into a ditch, getting hurt badly. The man called a doctor, who suggested using Goat lungs to heal the Ass. So, they killed the Goat to help the Ass.

This fable teaches us that sometimes jealousy can lead to bad consequences for others.

The Town Mouse and the Country Mouse

A Country Mouse invited his friend, a Town Mouse, to visit him. They ate simple food like wheat-stalks and roots. The Town Mouse said, "You live a boring life here! Come to my house, where I have plenty of delicious food." The Country Mouse agreed and went to the town.

At the Town Mouse's house, there were tasty treats like bread, beans, and cheese. But just as they started eating, someone came in, and they had to hide quickly in a tiny hole. They barely resumed their meal when another person came, and they had to run away again. The Country Mouse finally said, "I can't enjoy this food with so many dangers around. I'd rather go back to my simple, safe life."

This story teaches that it's better to be safe and content than to risk everything for luxury.

The Wolf, the Fox, and the Ape

A Wolf accused a Fox of stealing something. The Fox denied it, saying he was innocent. An Ape came to settle the argument. After hearing both sides, the Ape said, "I don't believe you, Wolf, ever lost what you claim, and I think you, Fox, have stolen what you deny."

This fable teaches us that dishonest people won't gain trust, even if they try to act honestly.

The Fly and the Draught-Mule

A Fly was sitting on the axle of a chariot and said to a Draught-Mule, "Why are you going so slow? I could sting you to make you go faster!" The Draught-Mule replied, "I don't care about your threats. I listen to the driver above me who uses the whip to speed me up or the reins to slow me down. You can buzz all you want, but I know when to go fast or slow."

This fable teaches that those in power are the ones who really control things, not those who just make noise.

The Fishermen

Some fishermen were out with their nets and thought they had caught a lot of fish because the nets felt heavy. They danced with joy, expecting a big catch. When they pulled the nets ashore, they found only a few fish, filled instead with sand and stones. Disappointed, one old fisherman said, "Let's stop being sad. It's normal for joy to be followed by sadness. We were too happy, so it makes sense that we now feel down."

This story reminds us that life is full of ups and downs.

The Lion and the Three Bulls

Three Bulls grazed together in a field. A hungry Lion wanted to catch them but was too afraid to attack while they stayed together. Eventually, the Lion tricked them into separating. Then he attacked them one by one and enjoyed his feast.

This fable teaches that there is strength in unity; when we stick together, we are safer.

The Fowler and the Viper

A Fowler was out to catch birds and was focused on a thrush in a tree. While he was busy watching, he accidentally stepped on a sleeping Viper. The Viper turned and bit him. As the Fowler fell, he realized, "Oh no! While I was trying to catch a bird, I ended up in danger myself!"

This fable teaches us to be aware of our surroundings, as danger can come when we least expect it.

The Horse and the Ass

One day, a proud Horse met a heavily loaded Ass on the road. The Horse boasted, "I could easily kick you aside!" The Ass remained quiet and silently hoped for justice. Later, the Horse became weak and was sent to work on a farm, pulling a dung cart. The Ass saw him and said, "Where are your fancy decorations now, proud Horse? Look at you, reduced to doing hard work like I did!"

This fable teaches that pride can lead to downfall, and those who look down on others may find themselves in a similar situation.

The Fox and the Mask

A Fox sneaked into an actor's home and found a beautiful Mask that looked like a human face. The Fox admired it and said, "What a lovely head! But it's useless because it has no brains!"

This story reminds us that appearances can be deceiving; beauty without substance has little value.

The Geese and the Cranes

In a meadow, Geese and Cranes were eating when a birdcatcher arrived to trap them. The light and quick Cranes flew away to safety, but the heavier Geese couldn't escape in time and were caught.

This fable teaches us that being light and agile can be an advantage in difficult situations.

The Blind Man and the Whelp

A Blind Man could tell animals apart by touch. One day, he was given a Wolf pup to feel. He said, "I can't tell if this is a Fox or a Wolf, but I know one thing: it's not safe to let him near the sheep!"

This story shows that bad tendencies can be present from a young age.

The Dogs and the Fox

Some Dogs found a Lion's skin and started tearing it apart. A Fox saw them and said, "If this Lion were alive, you would learn that his claws are much stronger than your teeth!"

This fable teaches that it's easy to bully someone who is already down or weak.

The Cobbler Turned Doctor

A Cobbler was struggling to make a living, so he decided to pretend to be a doctor in a new town. He sold a medicine, claiming it could cure all poisons, and became famous for his tall tales. One day, he fell seriously ill, and the town's Governor wanted to test his skills. He filled a cup with water, pretending to add poison, and told the Cobbler to drink it for a reward. Terrified, the Cobbler admitted he knew nothing about medicine and was only popular because of the crowd's foolishness. The Governor then told the townspeople, "How could you trust someone who couldn't even make shoes?"

This fable teaches us that we should be careful whom we trust, especially when it comes to important matters like health.

The Wolf and the Horse

A Wolf met a Horse and said, "You should go to that field over there. It's full of delicious oats that I left just for you because I care about your happiness!" The Horse replied, "If oats were good for wolves, you wouldn't have let your stomach suffer while you praised my meal!"

This story teaches that people with a bad reputation may not be believed even if they try to do something good.

The Brother and the Sister

A Father had a handsome son and an ugly daughter. One day, they looked into a mirror together. The boy admired his looks, but the girl got upset, thinking he was making fun of her. She ran to their father to complain. He hugged them both and said, "I wish you would look in the mirror every day: you, my son, to remember to be kind and not spoil your looks with bad behavior, and you, my daughter, to focus on being good-hearted and making up for what you think you lack."

This fable teaches that inner beauty and virtues are just as important as outer beauty.

The Wasps, the Partridges, and the Farmer

The Wasps and the Partridges were very thirsty and asked a Farmer for water. They promised to repay him: the Partridges said they would help his vines grow better grapes, and the Wasps said they would scare away thieves with their stings. The Farmer replied, "I already have two oxen who do all that without making promises. It's better to give the water to them!"

This story teaches us that actions speak louder than words, and those who can help without asking for anything in return are more valuable.

The Crow and Mercury

A Crow got caught in a trap and prayed to Apollo to help him, promising to give him some frankincense as a thank-you. Once Apollo freed him, the Crow forgot his promise. Later, he got caught again and asked Mercury for help, making the same promise. Mercury appeared and said, "How can I trust you? You broke your promise to Apollo!"

This fable teaches us that we should keep our promises, as breaking them can make others doubt us.

The North Wind and the Sun

The North Wind and the Sun were arguing about who was stronger. They decided that whoever could get a traveler to take off his coat would win. The North Wind blew as hard as he could, but the traveler just wrapped his coat tighter. Then, the Sun shone warmly, and the traveler quickly took off his coat and even jumped into a stream to cool off.

This story teaches that kindness and warmth can achieve what force cannot.

The Two Men Who Were Enemies

Two men who hated each other were sailing on the same ship. They sat as far apart as possible. When a storm hit, one man asked the pilot which end of the ship would sink first. The pilot said it would likely be the front. The man replied, "I wouldn't mind dying as long as I could see my enemy go first!"

This fable teaches that hatred can lead to dark thoughts, even in dangerous situations.

The Gamecocks and the Partridge

A man had two fighting Gamecocks. One day, he found a tame Partridge and brought it home. The Gamecocks bullied the Partridge, making him feel sad and out of place. But then he saw the Gamecocks fighting each other and realized that if they couldn't even get along, he shouldn't worry about their treatment of him.

This story teaches us that sometimes we worry too much about our troubles when others have their own conflicts.

The Quack Frog

Once, a Frog came out of the marsh and claimed to be a great doctor who could heal all kinds of illnesses. A Fox asked, "How can you be a doctor when you can't even fix your own lame legs and wrinkly skin?"

This fable teaches us that one should not pretend to have skills they don't actually possess.

The Lion, the Wolf, and the Fox

A sick old Lion lay in his cave while all the animals visited him except for the Fox. The Wolf saw this as a chance to get the Fox in trouble and told the Lion that the Fox was disrespecting him. Just then, the Fox arrived and defended himself, saying, "I have traveled far to find a cure for you." When the Lion asked for the cure, the Fox cleverly replied, "You need to wear the skin of a flayed Wolf." The Wolf was captured and flayed, and the Fox smiled, saying, "You should have been kind instead of plotting against me!"

This story teaches that scheming against others can lead to one's own downfall.

The Dog's House

In winter, a Dog decided he needed a house to keep warm, so he curled up tightly. But when summer came, he stretched out comfortably and thought he was too big to need a house anymore. He realized it wasn't necessary to build one after all.

This fable reminds us that our needs can change with the seasons, and sometimes what seemed important isn't necessary later.

The Wolf and the Lion

One evening, a Wolf saw his shadow and thought it looked huge. He boasted, "With a size like this, I should be the King of the beasts, not the Lion!" But just then, a Lion attacked and killed him. The Wolf realized too late that thinking too highly of himself led to his doom.

This story teaches that being arrogant can lead to dangerous consequences.

The Birds, the Beasts, and the Bat

During a war between the Birds and the Beasts, a Bat chose to fight with whoever seemed to be winning. When peace returned, both sides rejected him for his dishonesty. Because of this, the Bat had to hide in the dark and now only comes out at night.

This fable teaches us that being untrustworthy can lead to being rejected by everyone.

The Spendthrift and the Swallow

A young man who spent all his money had only one nice cloak left. One day, he saw a Swallow flying around and thought it meant summer had come early. So, he sold his cloak. But soon, winter returned, and he found the Swallow frozen and dead. He lamented, "You caused me to lose everything by coming too early!"

This story warns us that rushing into decisions based on false signs can lead to regret.

The Fox and the Lion

A Fox came across a Lion in a cage and started insulting him. The Lion replied, "You aren't insulting me; it's my bad luck that has trapped me here."

This fable teaches that one should be cautious in mocking others, as circumstances can change quickly.

The Owl and the Birds

An Owl advised the Birds to pull up acorns before they sprouted because they would produce mistletoe, which is dangerous for them. She also warned them about flax seeds and a man with arrows that would fly faster than they could. The Birds ignored her warnings and thought she was mad. Later, when they faced trouble, they realized the Owl was wise, but she stopped giving advice and mourned their foolishness.

This story shows that wisdom is often recognized too late, and ignoring good advice can lead to trouble.

The Trumpeter Taken Prisoner

A Trumpeter was captured by the enemy while bravely leading his soldiers. He pleaded for his life, saying he hadn't harmed anyone and only had his trumpet. The captors replied, "That's exactly why we should punish you; your trumpet encourages others to fight!"

This fable reminds us that even those who don't fight directly can still influence others and face consequences for it.

The Ass in the Lion's Skin

An Ass wore a Lion's skin and roamed the forest, scaring other animals. When he tried to frighten a Fox, the Fox said, "I might have been scared if I hadn't heard you bray!"

This story teaches that appearances can be deceiving, and true identity is revealed by actions.

The Sparrow and the Hare

A Hare was caught by an eagle and cried like a child. A Sparrow mocked her, asking where her speed was. Suddenly, a hawk caught the Sparrow and killed him. As the Hare died, she said, "You laughed at my misfortune, but now you face the same fate!"

This fable reminds us not to mock others, as our circumstances can change in an instant.

The Flea and the Ox

A Flea asked an Ox why he let men mistreat him when he was so big and strong, while the Flea fed on them. The Ox replied, "I am cared for and loved by men, and their kindness makes it worth it." The Flea lamented, "But their kindness leads to my end!"

This story highlights the different experiences of creatures and shows that what benefits one may harm another.

The Goods and the Ills

Once, the Goods were driven out by the Ills, who were too numerous. The Goods went to Jupiter, asking for a way to be free of the Ills. Jupiter agreed, saying the Ills would come in groups, while the Goods would arrive one by one.

This is why troubles come in numbers, while good things come slowly and individually.

This fable teaches us that good things may take time and come slowly, but bad things can overwhelm us quickly if we're not careful.

The Dove and the Crow

A Dove in a cage was proudly boasting about her many young ones. A Crow heard her and said, "Stop bragging! The more chicks you have, the sadder you should be since they're all stuck in this cage."

This fable teaches us that sometimes having more doesn't mean happiness, especially if it comes with problems.

Mercury and the Workmen

A Workman accidentally dropped his axe into a river and was very sad. Mercury appeared and asked why he was crying. When the Workman told him, Mercury jumped into the water and brought up a golden axe. The Workman said it wasn't his. Mercury then brought up a silver axe, but again the Workman said it wasn't his. Finally, Mercury retrieved the Workman's axe, and pleased with his honesty, gave him both the golden and silver axes.

Hearing this, another Workman tried to trick Mercury by throwing his axe into the river on purpose. When Mercury brought up the golden axe, the greedy Workman claimed it was his. Mercury took back the golden axe and didn't help him retrieve his own.

This fable teaches that honesty is rewarded, while greed leads to loss.

The Eagle and the Jackdaw

An Eagle swooped down and caught a lamb in its talons. A Jackdaw, feeling jealous, wanted to be like the Eagle. He tried to catch a ram but got stuck in its thick fleece. The shepherd saw him and captured the Jackdaw. When his children asked what kind of bird it was, the father said, "He thinks he's an Eagle, but he's really just a Daw."

This story reminds us to be ourselves and not pretend to be something we're not, or we might get into trouble.

The Fox and the Crane

A Fox invited a Crane to dinner and served soup on a flat stone dish. The Crane couldn't eat any of it because it fell out of her long beak. The Fox laughed at her. Later, the Crane invited the Fox over and served food in a tall, narrow flask. The Fox couldn't drink anything, and the Crane got her revenge for the Fox's unkind hospitality.

This fable teaches that we should treat others the way we want to be treated and that unfairness will come back to us.

Jupiter, Neptune, Minerva, and Momus

In an ancient legend, Jupiter created the first man, Neptune made the first bull, and Minerva built the first house. They argued over who made the best creation and decided to let Momus judge their work. But Momus, who was very envious, found faults in everything.

He criticized Neptune for not placing the bull's horns below its eyes so it could see better. He told Jupiter that the heart of man should be on the outside so others could see his true feelings. Finally, he scolded Minerva for not using iron wheels in her house's foundation, which would help people move easily if they had to.

Angry at Momus's constant complaints, Jupiter kicked him out of Olympus.

This fable teaches us that constant criticism and envy can lead to isolation and rejection.

The Eagle and the Fox

An Eagle and a Fox became close friends and decided to live near each other. The Eagle built her nest in a tall tree, while the Fox settled in the bushes below. One day, when the Fox was out, the Eagle snatched one of the Fox's cubs to feed her own little eaglets.

When the Fox returned and discovered what happened, she was heartbroken but wanted revenge. Soon after, the Eagle flew near an altar where villagers were sacrificing a goat. She grabbed some meat and a burning ember to take back to her nest. The ember ignited, and her eaglets were caught in the fire and died. The Fox then ate the eaglets that fell to the ground.

This story reminds us that betrayal can lead to consequences, and those who harm others may end up suffering themselves.

The Man and the Satyr

A Man and a Satyr decided to become friends and drank together. One cold winter day, the Man blew on his fingers to warm them up. The Satyr asked why he did that, and the Man explained it was to warm his hands. Later, when they sat down to eat, the food was too hot. The Man blew on the dish to cool it down.

The Satyr became upset and said, "I can't be friends with someone who blows both hot and cold."

This fable teaches us that being inconsistent can lead to misunderstandings in relationships, and it's important to be sincere and straightforward.

The Ass and His Purchaser

A man wanted to buy an Ass and decided to try it out first. He took the Ass home and put it with his other Asses. The new Ass immediately chose to hang out with the laziest and hungriest one. Seeing this, the man led the new Ass back to its owner. When asked why he returned so quickly, he replied, "I don't need to try it out; I know he'll be just like the lazy one he chose to be with."

This fable teaches that people are often judged by the company they keep.

The Two Bags

According to an old legend, every person is born with two bags: one in front, filled with their neighbours' faults, and one behind, filled with their own faults. This is why people are quick to notice others' mistakes but often overlook their own.

The lesson here is to be aware of our own faults instead of only pointing out the faults of others.

The Stag at the Pool

One hot day, a Stag went to a spring to drink water. While drinking, he saw his reflection and admired his beautiful antlers but felt upset about his thin, weak legs. Suddenly, a Lion appeared, and the Stag ran away. He managed to escape across the open plain, but when he entered the woods, his antlers got stuck in the branches. The Lion caught him, and the Stag regretted his earlier thoughts, saying, "Oh no! I valued my antlers and neglected my legs, which could have saved me."

This fable reminds us that what we often undervalue may be the most important.

The Jackdaw and the Fox

A hungry Jackdaw sat on a fig tree, hoping to find some figs, even though they weren't in season. A Fox saw him and said, "You're wasting your time hoping for figs that won't ripen. You're just deceiving yourself."

This story teaches that sometimes we hope for things that are unrealistic and that we should be more practical.

The Lark Burying Her Father

The Lark, according to an ancient story, was created before the earth. When her father died, there was no earth to bury him. For five days, she left him unburied. Finally, not knowing what else to do, she buried him in her own head, which is why Larks have crests today, said to be their father's grave.

This fable emphasizes the importance of respecting and honouring our parents.

The Gnat and the Bull

A Gnat landed on a Bull's horn and stayed for a while. Before leaving, the Gnat buzzed and asked the Bull if he would like him to go. The Bull replied, "I didn't even know you were here, and I won't miss you when you're gone."

This story teaches us that some people think they are more important than they really are to others.

The Bitch and Her Whelps

A mother dog was about to have puppies and asked a shepherd for a safe place to have them. The shepherd agreed and even let her raise her puppies there. But as the puppies grew up and became strong, the mother dog claimed the place as her own and wouldn't let the shepherd come near anymore.

This fable teaches that some may take advantage of kindness once they become strong.

The Dogs and the Hides

Some hungry dogs saw cowhides soaking in a river but couldn't reach them. They decided to drink up the river to get to the hides. However, they drank too much water and burst their bellies before they could reach the hides.

This story warns us not to attempt impossible tasks.

The Shepherd and the Sheep

A shepherd was taking his sheep to a wood and saw a big oak tree full of acorns. He spread his cloak under the tree and climbed up to shake the acorns down. While the sheep were eating the acorns, they accidentally tore his cloak. When he came down and saw what they had done, he said, "You ungrateful creatures! You provide wool for others, but you ruin my clothes!"

This fable reminds us to appreciate those who take care of us.

The Grasshopper and the Owl

An Owl, who slept during the day and hunted at night, was disturbed by a noisy Grasshopper. The Owl asked her to stop chirping, but the Grasshopper just got louder. Frustrated, the Owl came up with a plan. She said, "Since I can't sleep because of your sweet song, I'll drink some nectar. Would you like to join me?" The curious Grasshopper flew over, and the Owl seized her and killed her.

This story teaches us that those who boast about their talents may find themselves in danger.

The Monkey and the Camel

The animals of the forest held a big party, and the Monkey performed a fun dance that made everyone cheer. Envious of the Monkey's applause, the Camel wanted to dance too. However, when he tried, he moved in such a silly way that the other animals became angry and chased him away with sticks.

This fable teaches us that it's foolish to try to imitate those who are better than us.

The Peasant and the Apple-Tree

A peasant had an apple tree in his garden that didn't produce any fruit. Instead, it only attracted grasshoppers and sparrows. Deciding to cut it down, he swung his axe at the tree. The grasshoppers and sparrows pleaded for him to spare it, promising to sing for him. Ignoring them, he kept chopping until he discovered a hive filled with honey inside the tree. After tasting the honey, he decided to take care of the tree instead of cutting it down.

This story shows that some people act out of self-interest, not kindness.

The Two Soldiers and the Robber

Two soldiers were traveling together when a robber attacked them. One soldier ran away, while the other bravely fought back and defeated the robber. When the timid soldier came back, he drew his sword and boasted about how he would have fought the robber. The soldier who fought replied, "I wish you had helped me when I needed it, even with just words of encouragement. But now, keep your sword sheathed and your mouth shut, because I know you won't help in a crisis."

This fable reminds us that bravery is shown through actions, not words.

The Trees Under the Protection of the Gods

The gods chose certain trees to protect. Jupiter picked the oak, Venus chose the myrtle, Apollo selected the laurel, Cybele liked the pine, and Hercules favored the poplar. Minerva wondered why they picked trees that didn't bear fruit. Jupiter replied that they didn't want to seem greedy for fruit. Minerva argued that she preferred the olive tree because of its fruit. Jupiter agreed, saying, "You're right; what we do should be useful, or it's not worth much."

This story teaches us that true worth lies in usefulness rather than appearance.

The Mother and the Wolf

A hungry Wolf was looking for food when he heard a mother telling her child, "Be quiet, or I'll throw you out for the Wolf to eat!" The Wolf waited all day by the door, but later, he heard the mother say sweetly, "You're quiet now, and if the Wolf comes, we'll kill him!" The Wolf went home cold and empty, and when asked why he returned without food, he said, "I was foolish to believe the words of a woman!"

This fable warns us not to trust everything we hear.

The Ass and the Horse

AN ASS besought a Horse to spare him a small portion of his feed. "Yes," said the Horse; "if any remains out of what I am now eating I will give it you for the sake of my own superior dignity, and if you will come when I reach my own stall in the evening, I will give you a little sack full of barley." The Ass replied, "Thank you. But I can't think that you, who refuse me a little matter now, will by and by confer on me a greater benefit."

Moral: Don't trust those who refuse you small favors.

Truth and the Traveller

A WAYFARING MAN, traveling in the desert, met a woman standing alone and terribly dejected. He inquired of her, "Who art thou?" "My name is Truth," she replied. "And for what cause," he asked, "have you left the city to dwell alone here in the wilderness?" She made answer, "Because in former times, falsehood was with few, but is now with all men."

Moral: Truth is often abandoned for lies.

The Manslayer

A MAN committed a murder and was pursued by the relations of the man whom he murdered. On his reaching the river Nile, he saw a Lion on its bank and, being fearfully afraid, climbed up a tree. He found a serpent in the upper branches of the tree and, again being greatly alarmed, he threw himself into the river, where a crocodile caught him and ate him. Thus the earth, the air, and the water alike refused shelter to a murderer.

Moral: No refuge can be found for the guilty.

The Lion and the Fox

A FOX entered into partnership with a Lion on the pretense of becoming his servant. Each undertook his proper duty in accordance with his own nature and powers. The Fox discovered and pointed out the prey; the Lion sprang on it and seized it. The Fox soon became jealous of the Lion carrying off the Lion's share and said that he would no longer find out the prey but would capture it on his own account. The next day he attempted to snatch a lamb from the fold, but he himself fell prey to the huntsmen and hounds.

Moral: Jealousy can lead to one's downfall.

The Lion and the Eagle

AN EAGLE stayed his flight and entreated a Lion to make an alliance with him to their mutual advantage. The Lion replied, "I have no objection, but you must excuse me for requiring you to find surety for your good faith, for how can I trust anyone as a friend who is able to fly away from his bargain whenever he pleases?"

Moral: Try before you trust.

The Hen and the Swallow

A HEN finding the eggs of a viper and carefully keeping them warm, nourished them into life. A Swallow, observing what she had done, said, "You silly creature! Why have you hatched these vipers which, when they shall have grown, will inflict injury on all, beginning with yourself?"

Moral: Beware of nurturing harmful things.

The Buffoon and the Countryman

A RICH NOBLEMAN once opened the theatres without charge to the people and gave a public notice that he would handsomely reward any person who invented a new amusement for the occasion. Various public performers contended for the prize. Among them came a Buffoon well known among the populace for his jokes and said that he had a kind of entertainment which had never been brought out on any stage before. This report being spread about made a great stir, and the theatre was crowded in every part.

The Buffoon appeared alone upon the platform, without any apparatus or confederates, and the very sense of expectation caused an intense silence. He suddenly bent his head towards his bosom and imitated the squeaking of a little pig so admirably with his voice that the audience declared he had a porker under his cloak and demanded that it should be shaken out. When that was done and nothing was found, they cheered the actor and loaded him with the loudest applause.

A Countryman in the crowd, observing all that had passed, said, "So help me, Hercules, he shall not beat me at that trick!" and at once proclaimed that he would do the same thing on the next day, though in a much more natural way.

On the morrow, a still larger crowd assembled in the theatre, but now partiality for their favourite actor very generally prevailed, and the audience came rather to ridicule the Countryman than to see the spectacle. Both of the performers appeared on the stage. The Buffoon grunted and squeaked away first and obtained, as on the preceding day, the applause and cheers of the spectators.

Next, the Countryman commenced, and pretending that he concealed a little pig beneath his clothes (which in truth he did, but not suspected by the audience), contrived to take hold of and to pull his ear, causing the pig to squeak. The crowd, however, cried out with one consent that the Buffoon had given a far more exact imitation and clamoured for the Countryman to be kicked out of the theatre.

On this, the rustic produced the little pig from his cloak and showed by the most positive proof the greatness of their mistake. "Look here," he said, "this shows what sort of judges you are."

Moral: Don't be quick to judge based on appearances.

The Crow and the Serpent

A CROW in great want of food saw a Serpent asleep in a sunny nook, and flying down, greedily seized him. The Serpent, turning about, bit the Crow with a mortal wound. In the agony of death, the bird exclaimed: "O unhappy me! who have found in that which I deemed a happy windfall the source of my destruction."

Moral: Sometimes what seems like a blessing can lead to our downfall.

The Hunter and the Horseman

A CERTAIN HUNTER, having snared a hare, placed it upon his shoulders and set out homewards. On his way, he met a man on horseback who begged the hare of him under the pretence of purchasing it. However, when the Horseman got the hare, he rode off as fast as he could. The Hunter ran after him, as if he was sure of overtaking him, but the Horseman increased more and more the distance between them. The Hunter, sorely against his will, called out to him and said, "Get along with you! for I will now make you a present of the hare."

Moral: Don't be fooled by deceitful appearances.

The King's Son and the Painted Lion

A KING, whose only son was fond of martial exercises, had a dream in which he was warned that his son would be killed by a lion. Afraid the dream should prove true, he built for his son a pleasant palace and adorned its walls with all kinds of life-sized animals, among which was the picture of a lion. When the young Prince saw this, his grief at being thus confined burst out afresh, and, standing near the lion, he said: "O you most detestable of animals! Through a lying dream of my father's, which he saw in his sleep, I am shut up on your account in this palace as if I had been a girl: what shall I now do to you?"

With these words, he stretched out his hands toward a thorn-tree, meaning to cut a stick from its branches so that he might beat the lion. But one of the tree's prickles pierced his finger and caused great pain and inflammation, so that the young Prince fell down in a fainting fit. A violent fever suddenly set in, from which he died not many days later.

The Curious Cat and Venus

Once upon a time, in a sunny village, there lived a sweet little cat who dreamed of love. She spotted a handsome young man and wished to be just like him! So, she asked the magical goddess Venus for a special favor. "Oh, dear Venus, could you please turn me into a beautiful girl so that I can win his heart?"

With a twinkle in her eye, Venus granted her wish, and poof! The cat transformed into a lovely young lady. The handsome young man saw her and fell in love at first sight. He brought her home as his bride, and they spent happy days together.

One evening, as they relaxed in their cozy room, Venus wanted to see if the cat had truly changed. So, she dropped a little mouse in the middle of the room! The cat, forgetting she was now a girl, jumped up with excitement, chasing after the mouse, her old instincts kicking in!

Venus chuckled, realizing that some things never change. With a smile, she turned the cat back into her furry self. "It seems," she said with a wink, "that a cat will always be a cat!"

The Goats and Their Beards

In a cheerful meadow, a group of playful she-goats decided they wanted to look just as grand as the he-goats. So, they asked Jupiter, the king of the gods, for some beards. "Please, let us have beards too!" they bleated, wanting to feel important.

Jupiter chuckled and granted their wish. The she-goats proudly wore their new beards, but the he-goats weren't too happy about it. "Hey! That's not fair!" they complained.

Jupiter laughed and said, "Let them enjoy their new beards! It's just a fun look. They might look like you, but remember, it's what's inside that truly matters!"

And so, the goats learned that while they could look alike on the outside, it was their unique qualities that made each of them special.

The Clever Camel and the Arab

In a bustling desert, a clever camel was getting ready for a long journey. His owner, an Arab camel-driver, loaded him up with supplies and asked, "Hey, my friend, would you rather go uphill or downhill?"

The wise camel thought for a moment and replied, "Why ask me? Wouldn't it be easier to just stroll along the flat desert path?"

The driver chuckled, realizing that no matter the path, their adventure together would be filled with fun and laughter. And off they went, exploring the vast, sandy world side by side, where every journey was an exciting story waiting to unfold!

The Miller, His Son, and Their Funny Ass

Once upon a time, in a cheerful little village, there lived a kind miller and his playful son. One sunny morning, they decided to take their fluffy ass to the nearby fair to sell him.

As they walked along the dusty road, they came across a group of giggling ladies chatting around a well.

"Look at those two!" one of the ladies exclaimed. "Why are they walking when they could be riding?" Hearing this, the miller thought it was a great idea. He quickly helped his son hop onto the ass, and off they went, the son smiling from the comfy seat while the miller walked beside him.

Before long, they met a group of wise old men who were deep in discussion. "Look at that young lad riding while his poor father walks!" one of the old men declared. "What a shame! Youngsters today don't respect their elders!" The miller, wanting to make everyone happy, told his son to hop off and let him have a turn riding the ass.

They continued on their journey when they bumped into a bunch of women and children. "Oh my, you lazy man!" they said, pointing. "How can you ride while that poor little boy has to walk?" The miller, always ready to please, lifted his son up behind him, and now they both rode together!

As they got closer to town, a friendly citizen called out, "Is that ass yours?" "Yes!" replied the miller proudly. "Well, it looks like you're loading him up with too much!" the citizen laughed. "Why, you two are better off carrying him than he is carrying you!"

Feeling adventurous and wanting to impress everyone, the miller and his son hopped off the ass. They tied his legs with a rope, grabbed a pole, and tried to lift the poor creature onto their shoulders. The sight of them carrying their ass made everyone burst into laughter!

But the silly ass didn't like being lifted like that. With a quick wiggle, he broke free from the ropes and tumbled off the pole, splashing right into the river with a big *splash!*

The miller, feeling a bit embarrassed but still chuckling, decided it was best to head home. He realized that by trying to please everyone, he ended up pleasing no one and lost his silly ass in the process.

From that day on, he learned to enjoy the simple moments and be happy just as they were!

The Cheerful Crow and the Friendly Sheep

Once upon a time, a cheeky Crow decided to perch on the back of a fluffy Sheep. The Sheep was not too happy about this, but he carried the Crow around for a while. Finally, the Sheep said, "If you tried this with a dog, he would give you a little bite for your trouble!" The Crow laughed and replied, "Oh, I like to play with the ones who are gentle, and I know how to be sweet to the strong! That's how I enjoy a long, happy life!"

The Fox and the Prickly Bramble

One sunny day, a clever Fox was trying to jump over a hedge but slipped and grabbed onto a prickly Bramble to save himself. Ouch! The Bramble poked him, and the Fox exclaimed, "Why would you hurt me when I needed help?" The Bramble chuckled and said, "Oh dear Fox, you should know I'm always a little prickly! You shouldn't have grabbed onto someone like me!"

The Wolf and the Brave Lion

One day, a sneaky Wolf had stolen a fluffy lamb and was strutting along when a mighty Lion appeared. The Lion swiftly took the lamb away from him. The Wolf whined, "That's mine! You shouldn't take it!" The Lion smirked and replied, "Oh really? Is it yours, or was it just a little gift from your friend the sheep?"

The Hungry Dog and the Sneaky Oyster

Once, there was a hungry Dog who loved eggs. One day, he spotted an Oyster and thought it was the biggest egg ever! With a big gulp, he swallowed it down, but oh no! His tummy began to hurt! He groaned, "I should've been careful! Not everything round is an egg!" And from that day, he learned to think twice before gobbling things up!

The Ant and the Kind Dove

One hot day, a thirsty Ant waddled to a river for a drink. Suddenly, a big wave swept him away, and he was in trouble! A kind Dove sitting in a tree saw this and dropped a leaf into the water. The Ant climbed on and floated safely to the shore. Later, when a sneaky birdcatcher came to catch the Dove, the Ant noticed and stung the catcher's foot. Ouch! The birdcatcher dropped his trap, and the Dove flew away safely, all thanks to the brave little Ant!

The Partridge and the Generous Fowler

One day, a kind Fowler caught a Partridge and was about to take him home. The Partridge pleaded, "Please spare my life! If you let me go, I can bring many friends to you!" The Fowler thought for a moment and said, "I'm afraid I can't trust you if you're willing to betray your friends. But I admire your cleverness!" And with that, he let the Partridge fly free, knowing that friendship is more valuable than a quick catch!

The Playful Flea and the Laughing Man

In a cozy little house, a Man was very annoyed with a tiny Flea that kept hopping around. Finally, he caught the Flea and said, "Who do you think you are, bothering me like this?" The Flea replied, "Oh, please spare me! I'm too small to cause you trouble!" The Man chuckled and said, "Maybe you are tiny, but even the little ones can be pesky! However, I think I'll let you go this time!" And with a smile, he released the Flea, learning that sometimes even the smallest friends can bring the biggest joys!

The Thieves and the Clever Cock

One night, some mischievous Thieves sneaked into a house, but all they found was a loud and proud Cock! They decided to take him home with them. When they got there, the Cock pleaded, "Please don't hurt me! I wake everyone up in the morning to start their day!"

The Thieves laughed and said, "That's exactly why we can't keep you alive! If you wake everyone up, we can't do our sneaky work!"

And so, the Cock realized that sometimes, being helpful can make you a target for those with bad intentions!

The Dog and the Festive Feast

Once, a wealthy man threw a grand feast and invited all his friends. His playful Dog saw this as a perfect chance to invite his buddy, a stray Dog. "Come join me! My master always has leftover food!" he said.

The stray Dog arrived, wagging his tail in excitement. "Wow! Look at all this food! I'll eat enough for today and tomorrow!" But just as he was munching happily, the Cook spotted him and quickly tossed him out the window!

The poor Dog landed on the ground, limping and howling. Soon, other street dogs gathered around and asked, "How was the feast?" The stray Dog sighed, "Honestly, I drank too much wine and don't remember a thing! I just know I had a rough exit!"

The Travellers and the Grateful Plane-Tree

On a hot summer day, two weary travellers found a big, shady Plane-Tree and rested beneath its cool branches. One traveller sighed, "What a useless tree! It doesn't bear any fruit or do anything for us!"

Just then, the Plane-Tree spoke up, "Ungrateful Travellers! While you enjoy my shade, you call me useless? How can you say that?"

The travellers were taken aback, realizing how wrong they were to underestimate the tree that was providing them comfort. Sometimes, we don't appreciate the blessings we have right in front of us!

The Hares and the Timid Frogs

In a meadow, the Hares were feeling very scared and tired of being jumpy all the time. They decided they would rather leap off a high cliff into the lake below than continue living in fear. As they hopped toward the cliff, they startled a group of Frogs lounging by the water.

Seeing the Frogs jump into the lake in a panic, one Hare stopped and called out, "Wait! Look at those Frogs! They're even more scared than we are! Maybe we shouldn't be so quick to give up!"

And so, the Hares realized that there are always others who might be feeling even more scared than they are, and they decided to keep hopping instead of jumping!

The Lion, Jupiter, and the Wise Elephant

Once upon a time, a mighty Lion was feeling a bit sorry for himself. He went to Jupiter, the king of the gods, and complained, "Oh, Jupiter! I'm big and strong, with sharp teeth and claws, yet I'm scared of a little Cock's crowing! How embarrassing!"

Jupiter, with a knowing smile, replied, "But my friend, I've given you all my best gifts! You're brave in many ways, except when it comes to that pesky crow. Why dwell on it?"

Feeling sad, the Lion wandered into the forest and met a big, gentle Elephant. Curious, the Lion asked, "Why do you keep shaking your ears?"

The Elephant sighed and pointed at a tiny Gnat buzzing around. "If that little bug gets into my ear, I could be in big trouble!"

The Lion looked at the Elephant and thought, "If such a huge creature can be afraid of such a tiny thing, then I shouldn't feel so bad about my own fears!"

From that day on, the Lion learned that everyone has their worries, no matter how strong or big they are!

The Lamb and the Clever Wolf

One sunny day, a sly Wolf spotted a little Lamb and chased after him. The frightened Lamb ran straight to a nearby Temple for safety. The Wolf called out, "You better watch out! The Priest will catch you and use you for a sacrifice!"

The clever Lamb replied, "Well, I'd rather be a sacrifice in the Temple than be eaten by you! At least I would have a noble end!"

The Wolf, realizing the Lamb was smarter than he looked, decided to rethink his plan.

The Rich Man and the Patient Tanner

In a bustling town, a Rich Man lived next to a Tanner who worked hard every day. The Rich Man hated the unpleasant smell from the Tanner's yard. "Oh, you must move away!" he complained.

The Tanner smiled and said, "I'll move soon, I promise!" But he kept staying, and as time passed, the Rich Man got used to the smell and forgot all about his complaints.

Eventually, he realized that sometimes, we can adapt to things that once bothered us!

The Shipwrecked Man and the Wise Sea

Once upon a time, a Shipwrecked Man washed up on a beautiful shore after a wild adventure at sea. Exhausted from his struggles with the waves, he fell asleep on the warm sand. When he woke up, he looked out at the calm Sea and shouted, "How could you be so cruel? You trick people with your peaceful looks, only to turn into a monster and drown them!"

Suddenly, the Sea transformed into a graceful woman and replied, "Oh dear friend, don't blame me! I am usually calm and gentle, just like the earth. It's the wild winds that make me wave and roar. They come out of nowhere and stir me into a frenzy!"

The man listened carefully and realized that sometimes, things aren't what they seem. The winds were the real troublemakers!

The Mules and the Clever Grain Mule

Two Mules were walking along a dusty path, each carrying heavy loads. One Mule carried shiny gold and coins, while the other carried sacks of grain. The gold-carrying Mule strutted proudly, making sure everyone could hear the jingle of the coins. Meanwhile, the grain Mule walked quietly and calmly.

Suddenly, a group of Robbers jumped out from behind the bushes! They fought with the Mules' owners and, in the chaos, hurt the Mule with the treasure and stole all the gold. The grain Mule watched in relief as his friend cried out, "Oh no! My treasure!"

The grain Mule replied, "I'm actually glad I carried something less valuable. I'm safe and sound, while you're left with nothing but a wound!"

Sometimes, it's better to be underestimated than to carry a heavy burden!

The Viper and the File

One day, a hungry Lion wandered into a busy blacksmith's workshop, looking for something to eat. He approached a shiny File and said, "Hey there, can you help me out? I'm quite hungry!"

The File chuckled and replied, "Oh, you must be a bit confused! I'm not the one to help you—I'm always taking from others, not giving! You'll get nothing from me!"

The Lion realized that not everything is as helpful as it seems, and he moved on in search of a meal.

The Lion and the Kind Shepherd

In a dense forest, a Lion was strolling when he stepped on a thorn! Ouch! He hopped around, feeling the sharp pain. Soon, he spotted a kind Shepherd nearby. The Lion approached him, wagging his tail and asking for help.

The Shepherd, a brave soul, knelt down and examined the Lion's paw. "Don't worry, my friend! I'll help you!" he said, pulling out the thorn. The Lion felt much better and thanked the Shepherd before wandering back into the forest.

Later, the Shepherd found himself in trouble and was wrongly accused of a crime. He was sentenced to be thrown to the Lions! But when the cage door opened, the Lion recognized the Shepherd—the one who had helped him! Instead of attacking, the Lion approached and gently placed his paw on the Shepherd's lap.

The King, hearing this tale of kindness, decided to set both the Lion and the Shepherd free. They were grateful for their second chances and became the best of friends!

The Camel and Jupiter

Once upon a time, there was a Camel who looked at a Bull with magnificent horns and felt a twinge of jealousy. "Oh, how I wish I had horns like that!" the Camel exclaimed. So, he went to Jupiter, the king of the gods, and asked for horns of his own.

Jupiter scratched his head, a bit annoyed. "You're already strong and big, Camel! Why can't you be happy with what you have?" And with that, instead of giving the Camel horns, Jupiter took away a little bit of his ears!

From that day on, the Camel learned that it's best to appreciate what you have rather than wishing for what others possess.

The Panther and the Shepherds

One day, a Panther fell into a deep pit. The Shepherds found him and didn't know what to do! Some threw sticks and stones, thinking they'd drive him away, while others felt sorry for the trapped Panther and tossed in some food.

That night, the Shepherds went home, thinking the Panther would be gone by morning. But the clever Panther managed to escape and was very angry! He returned to find the Shepherds and, instead of attacking them all, he remembered who had harmed him and who had helped him.

To those who showed kindness, he said, "Don't worry! I remember who fed me and who threw stones." The Shepherds learned a valuable lesson that day about kindness and the consequences of their actions.

The Ass and the Brave Horse

An Ass saw a magnificent Horse who was well-fed and taken care of. "You're so lucky!" the Ass said. "I have to work hard just to find a little grass to munch on." But then, war broke out, and a soldier mounted the Horse, riding him into battle.

The brave Horse fought valiantly but was wounded and fell on the battlefield. The Ass, watching all this unfold, felt sorry for the Horse. "Oh dear," he said, "I take back what I said! It's not always easy to be a hero."

The Ass learned that sometimes it's tough being admired, and bravery comes with its own challenges.

The Eagle and His New Home

One sunny day, a proud Eagle was caught by a man who clipped his wings and kept him in a poultry yard. The Eagle felt so sad and trapped. Then, a kind neighbor bought the Eagle and let him grow his feathers back.

Once the Eagle regained his strength, he swooped down and caught a hare, bringing it as a gift to his new friend. But a sneaky Fox watched and warned, "Be careful! Don't forget your old owner who might try to catch you again!"

The Eagle learned that true friends are those who treat you well, and he made sure to stay close to those who helped him.

The Bald Man and the Teasing Fly

One day, a pesky Fly buzzed around and bit a Bald Man on the head. In his frustration, the Bald Man tried to swat the Fly but ended up slapping himself instead!

The Fly laughed and said, "Look what you did to yourself just because of a tiny bug!" The Bald Man chuckled back, "I can forgive myself, but oh how I wish I could catch you! You may be small, but you're such a bother!"

The Bald Man realized that sometimes little annoyances can lead to big laughs!

The Olive Tree and the Fig Tree

In a beautiful garden, an Olive Tree laughed at a Fig Tree for losing its leaves every autumn. "Look at me! I'm green all year round!" the Olive Tree boasted. But one winter, a heavy snow fell, and the Olive Tree couldn't bear the weight and broke its branches.

The Fig Tree, bare but sturdy, weathered the snow without a scratch. "Sometimes," said the Fig Tree with a smile, "it's better to be prepared than to show off!"

The Olive Tree learned that true strength comes from within, no matter the seasons.

The Eagle and the Kite

Once, a lonely Eagle perched high in a tree, looking sad. A Kite swooped down and asked, "Why so glum?" The Eagle replied, "I can't find a mate!" The Kite offered, "Choose me! I'm strong and can catch big meals!"

The Eagle, excited, agreed to take the Kite as her partner. But when it came time to prove his worth, the Kite returned with a tiny mouse instead of an ostrich!

"Is this the best you can do?" asked the disappointed Eagle. The Kite replied sheepishly, "I promised you the moon, but I guess I can only deliver a mouse!"

The Eagle learned that it's better to be honest than to make promises you can't keep.

The Ass and His Driver

One sunny day, an eager Ass was being led along a winding road when he suddenly decided to run off! He dashed toward a steep cliff, thinking of taking a big leap. Just as he was about to jump, his owner grabbed him by the tail, pulling with all his might.

"Stop, you silly creature!" the driver shouted. But the Ass was determined. "I want to fly!" he brayed, trying to shake free. Finally, the driver, tired and exasperated, let go and said, "Fine! Go ahead, but remember, you'll regret it!"

With a surprised look, the Ass tumbled down the cliff. "Oh no!" he realized. "Maybe I should have listened!"

The lesson here is that sometimes our desires can lead us into trouble, and it's wise to think twice before acting on them!

The Thrush and the Fowler

One bright afternoon, a delightful Thrush was perched on a myrtle tree, munching on the juiciest berries. "Yum! This is the best snack ever!" she chirped, staying longer than she should have.

A clever Fowler noticed her enjoying herself and thought, "What a perfect chance to catch that bird!" He set up his bird-limed reeds, and with a sly grin, he waited.

Suddenly, the Thrush felt something sticky on her feet. "Oh no! I'm trapped!" she cried. "Why did I stay for these yummy berries when my life was at stake?"

As the Fowler scooped her up, she learned a valuable lesson: sometimes, it's better to be cautious and leave the delicious treats behind than to risk losing everything.

The Rose and the Amaranth

In a beautiful garden, an Amaranth grew beside a radiant Rose. The Amaranth admired the Rose's vibrant colors and sweet scent. "Oh, how I wish I could be as lovely as you!" it said. "Everyone loves you!"

The Rose smiled kindly and replied, "Thank you, dear Amaranth! But remember, my beauty is only for a short time. I may be plucked today or wilt tomorrow. You, on the other hand, bloom forever and never fade."

The Amaranth thought for a moment and said, "You're right! I may not be as pretty, but I will always be here, growing strong."

And so, they both learned that true beauty comes in many forms, and lasting qualities are often more valuable than fleeting moments of glory.

The Frogs' Complaint against the Sun

One hot day, the Sun declared to all, "I'm ready to find a wife!" Upon hearing this, the Frogs in the marsh began to croak and complain loudly.

"Why are they so noisy?" Jupiter, the king of the gods, wondered as he looked down at the commotion. One brave Frog jumped forward and said, "Oh great Jupiter! If the Sun has a family, we'll surely suffer! He already dries up our marshes. What will happen if he has little suns to follow him?"

The Frogs worried and fretted about their future. Jupiter listened and promised, "I will keep a close watch on the Sun.

Don't worry; your voices are heard!"

The Frogs learned that sometimes, it's okay to speak up about your concerns, and those in power might just listen!

The Author

Dr. Anshumali Pandey: The Hospitality Guru, Tribal Food Enthusiast & Master of Many Hats

If there were a PhD in doing everything exceptionally well, Dr. Anshumali Pandey would probably have written the syllabus. A man of many talents (and possibly more hours in the day than the rest of us), he has seamlessly juggled roles as an educator, chef, author, business auditor, and culinary adventurer—all while maintaining an unwavering enthusiasm for tribal cuisine, tourism, and the hospitality industry.

Armed with a PhD in Management, Dr. Pandey has mastered the complex world of higher education, office administration, HR, labor laws, audits, procurement, and tender processes—essentially, all the things that make most people's heads spin. His expertise has rightfully earned him recognition from the Ministry of Tourism, Government of India, which awarded him a National Appreciation certificate and a memento in 2018 (presumably, for being an unstoppable force of knowledge and innovation).

His passion for tribal food and tourism isn't just a hobby—it's practically a second career. While most people collect fridge magnets from their travels, Dr. Pandey collects research papers, having published a staggering 99 works, including 78 books and short stories. His writing portfolio spans everything from culinary arts to HR management, children's literature to spirituality—because why stick to one genre when you can master them all?

For over two decades, he has lived in the picturesque tribal belt of Dadra & Nagar Haveli, dedicating his time to understanding and uplifting rural communities. If there's a story to be told about indigenous culture or a traditional recipe that needs preserving, Dr. Pandey is probably already writing about it.

A true hospitality sector powerhouse, Dr. Pandey's boundless passion, encyclopedic knowledge, and ability to make complicated subjects almost sound fun have cemented his reputation as an industry leader. His work continues to inspire aspiring professionals across multiple fields—though, honestly, just keeping up with his achievements is an accomplishment in itself!

Books written by the Author are –

1. Theory of Indian Cookery (2 Editions Printed)
2. Beauty and Irony of Silvassa Tourism
3. A Short Indian Food Story
4. Be Your Own Guide to Indian Cuisine
5. Cookery Fundamentals
6. History of Indian Food (2 Editions Printed)
7. The Great Indian Story Book for Children (Fiction)
8. Personal Budget: Easy Work Book

9. Online Classes Log Book
10. Dictionary Making Work Book for School Children
11. The Lazy Bed (Fiction)
12. Hindu Dharm (हिन्दू धर्म) (In Hindi Language)
13. Where is my coffee?
14. Your First Job is Never your Last (Volume 1)
15. You are Almost There (Quick Fix Resume and Interview Hacks)
16. Working for the Enemy? - A lesson in Career Management
17. Public Speaking for the Young
18. A Date With Coffee
19. How to be The Best Hotel Front Office Employee
20. Diploma in Food Production, The complete Syllabus
21. Diploma in F&B Service, The Complete Syllabus
22. Diploma in Front Office, The Complete Syllabus
23. The Time to Speak is Now
24. Munshi Premchand (Short Stories in English) (Fiction)
25. The Housekeeping Department, Text Book
26. Hitchhiker's Guide to Trekking in Uttarakhand
27. Uttarakhand, A divine Land for a Reason
28. Bachhon ke liye rochak kahaniyan (बच्चों के लिए रोचक कहानियाँ) (In Hindi Language) (Fiction)
29. Basic Communication Skills of English
30. The Basic Office Organisation Book for Start-ups
31. Hospitality HRM
32. Hospitality Marketing
33. Bakery Ingredients and Tools
34. Human Resource Management for Indian Professionals
35. The process of LAWFULLY operating a Hospitality business in India
36. Indian Classical Sweets: History, Tradition and Recipes

37. History of India's Himalayan Cuisine: Classical Cookery of Kashmir, Laddakh, Jammu, Himachal, Lahaul, Spiti, Garhwal, Kumaon.
38. Vindu: Andhra Cuisine (Part 1 of South Indian Trilogy)
39. Saappadu: Tamil Cuisine (Part 2 of South Indian Trilogy)
40. Sadya: Malayali Cuisine (Part 3 of South Indian Trilogy)
41. South Indian Cuisine - The Researcher's Guide Book
42. The Ramayana for Children and other short stories from Indian Mythology (Fiction)
43. Legends of the Tribal Shiva (Fiction)
44. Third Generation Children's Story Book (Fiction)
45. It's Elementary: The Top Nine Adventures from the memoirs of Dr John H Watson (2 Editions Printed) (Fiction)
46. UNITY IN DIVERSITY, The foundation of Indian Tourism
47. The Thar Express: Culinary History of Rajasthan and Gujarat
48. Basics of Computerized Accounting
49. Impact (Impact of Globalization on Indian Social Life)
50. Vishnu – The Lord of Amazing Incarnations (Fiction)
51. Being a Mahatma in the Freedom Struggle
52. The Culinary Journey of Purvanchal: Lucknow to Patna
53. Culinary History of the Gangetic Plains
54. Indian Culinary Secrets
55. The Story of Jain and Parsi Food
56. The Great Indian Pilgrimage Tourism
57. Introduction to Tourism Studies – Text Book
58. Bread and Rolls (2 Editions Printed)
59. Diploma in Digital Marketing the Complete Syllabus
60. The Theory of Sweetened Bakery Foods
61. Campus Placement Guide for Management Trainee in Leading Hotels

62. Diploma in Housekeeping Management, the Complete Syllabus
63. Jokes and Stories for Kids (Fiction)
64. Demigods of India (Fiction)
65. Practical Cookery Guide Book for Parents and School Teachers
66. Introduction to Cookery for Elementary School Children (Kindle)
67. The Fearless Entrepreneur (Being your own Boss)
68. Culinary Heritage of Bengal's Widow Culture
69. Journey into the Mythological Wisdom of Vedas & Puranas (Fiction)
70. From Stigma to Strength: The Legacy of Bengal's Widowhood
71. HAKKA: Discovering a Vibrant Community in India
72. The Indo Chinese Pot Boiler
73. Bombay Daak: Discovering the Kolis of the Seven Islands
74. Speak Your Mind: A Guide to Clear and Impactful Communication
75. Urbanization And Rural Dynamics In India
76. Short Stories from the Animal Kingdom (Fiction)
77. The Short Story Book for Children - Morals and Humour (Fiction)
78. Rivers of Justice (Fiction)

Connect with me: anshumali.pandey@gmail.com
https://notionpress.com/author/337004

Updated Information about the Author and his works